"I'd rath... what jus...happened."

Ariel's voice was tight with embarrassment. "I didn't mean to go so far."

"I see," he said after a long silence. "I suppose the rest of you is kept in cold storage for the mysterious Kane, when or if he ever deigns to come back. Is that it?"

"K-Kane?" she stammered, not sure she'd heard him properly.

In a shock, it suddenly dawned on her that not once during that passionate eruption did she imagine herself in the arms of Kane. The ghost had finally been exorcised from her heart. It was Chris Donahue who had broken through her defenses. Whether he wanted it or not, Chris had inherited all the stubborn, unreasonable love she had for Kane.

"Well, Ariel," he prompted, "where do we go from here?"

Natalie Spark made her first appearance in the Harlequin Romance line in July 1984 with *Once More with Feeling*. And anyone looking forward to a warm, intriguing romance with full-bodied characters will welcome the author's second romance novel, *One Life at a Time*.

Books by Natalie Spark

One Life at a Time

Natalie Spark

Harlequin Books

TORONTO • NEW YORK • LONDON
AMSTERDAM • PARIS • SYDNEY • HAMBURG
STOCKHOLM • ATHENS • TOKYO • MILAN

Original hardcover edition published in 1986
by Mills & Boon Limited

ISBN 0-373-02799-0

Harlequin Romance first edition November 1986

CHAPTER ONE

CHRIS DONAHUE was thoroughly fed up. He was not a patient man at the best of times but, he thought, this was too much even for the most equable man. He had spent the better part of two days cooped up in his London house, a reluctant referee to several eager candidates who were vying for a job which he considered an unnecessary nuisance in the first place. All of them came highly recommended and were perfectly suitable, of course, but the idea of being stuck with any one of them for weeks, even months, of close collaboration made him squirm with agitation.

'What a bloody waste of time,' he muttered, turning to his elderly agent who had been conducting the interviews for him. 'How many more do I have to see?'

'It's really up to you, Chris,' Paul Andrews answered shortly. He too had wasted two whole days, something he would have done for none of his other writers, and he was fast reaching the end of his tether. 'Any one of these script-writers would have been ideal. What the hell are you looking for? A human computer?'

'The less human the better,' his exasperated client agreed. 'Why don't we forget it, Paul?'

The elderly literary agent groaned wearily. 'Lay off, Chris. We've been over this time and time again. You may be a computer genius and a thrilling first-time novelist, but you can't just plunge into a film-script without any previous training or experience. You'll just have to collaborate with someone. Unless,' Paul continued cautiously, 'unless you leave the adaptation of the novel to a professional script-writer. That's what any sensible novelist would do if . . .' He faltered, defeated by the writer's cold blue gaze.

'I'm not a novelist,' Chris explained patiently. 'God only knows what made me write that one book in the first place. Nevertheless, I refuse to see my creation, pathetic as it is, rubbed and smoothed and polished into the old trite science fantasy formula. I either work on the script myself or we just scrap the film!'

'Oh all right.' The agent gave in. 'Have it your own way, Chris. I really don't know why I bother.'

They both knew perfectly well why he did. *The Island of the Lost* was Paul Andrews Literary Agency's most exciting property in recent years. It had been snapped up practically unread by publishers on both sides of the ocean and film producers had been clamouring for the film rights ever since, topping each other's offers of best directors, most illustrious stars, astronomical fees and unprecedented royalties. In all his years as a literary agent, Paul Andrews had never experienced such a race after a first-time, untried novelist, though both agent and his sardonic client were well aware that it was not the book's unquestionable literary merit which precipitated such a stormy interest but the writer's name.

Chris Donahue had been something of a legend in the computer world ever since he emerged as a precocious genius of seventeen to become the head of an international computer empire before reaching thirty; an unpredictable, enigmatic whiz-kid forever astounding his admirers and rivals with spectacular business coups as well as the hair-raising adventures in his private life. Nevertheless, as far as the general public was concerned, he remained as anonymous and faceless as most workaholic empire-builders until his private jet crashed somewhere in the Indian Ocean and he was written off for dead.

The aura of romance and mystery which shrouded the untimely death of the young dare-devil millionaire appealed to the press, and the public soon fell in love with his memory. The supposedly late Chris Donahue became an international celebrity, a subject of numerous articles and one hurriedly concocted inaccurate biography. One resourceful producer was even beginning to work on a film project.

And then, some six months after the crash, Chris

Donahue suddenly re-emerged from the land of the dead, without a word of explanation, contemptuously shunning the public's delighted clamour, refusing to resume his position as head of the Donahue empire and turning his back on his old way of life to retreat to some secret tropical haven. Naturally, the romantic imagination of the public was tickled even further by the curious transformation of the playboy into an enigmatic recluse. It was small wonder, then, that when he came out with a first book, a science fantasy, publishers and film moguls fell over each other in their eagerness to grab it. *The Island of the Lost* had all the makings of a box-office gold-mine.

The subject of all this bubbling excitement was utterly unmoved by it all. In fact, he had come to regret his rash decision to have the book published. He was impervious to money and resented the infringement on his privacy which all this hullabaloo had brought upon him. His agent now studied his long, lean, muscular frame sprawled in the Eames lounger, and his heart sank as he saw the clean-cut, handsome features set in an all-too-familiar mask of cold obstinacy.

'I'll see only one more candidate,' the writer announced flatly, a steely uncompromising edge dulling the low attractive resonance of his voice. 'And that's that.'

'And if this one doesn't come up to your vague expectations of the perfect collaborator, what then?'

'Then you can tell your chap, what's-his-name . . .'

'Peter Garland.' The agent supplied the name of the country's most celebrated film producer. 'And most writers would give their right arm just to have him consider their book . . .'

Chris wasn't impressed. 'You can tell him he either goes by my own "raw" adaptation or he can forget about the film rights.'

Paul Andrews shrugged his heavy body into a dark blue cashmere coat. 'I give up. It's useless arguing with you. And I must be off now, you'll have to conduct the next interview without me.'

'I'm damned if I will, Paul,' Chris Donahue fumed. 'You don't expect me to ask all those ridiculous questions myself, do you?'

'Sorry, but I must. I've been holding your hand for two days now and I can't keep away from the office any longer. You're not the only writer in my agency, you know. Just give me a call later on and tell me how she came out.'

'Oh, so it's a she, is it?'

Paul Andrews bristled, piqued by the writer's disdainful tone. 'What if it is? She's a perfect gem. What's more, she has no pretensions to being a script-writer. In fact, she's a production secretary who's specialised in working with script-writers, so that she knows all the technical ins and outs but won't bother you with her creative aspirations. Isn't that what you wanted?'

The hard, handsome face remained impassive. 'Young?'

The agent shuffled uneasily. 'Well, yes. Twenty-one, or thereabouts.'

'Married?'

'No, she isn't but I think she's got some chap stashed away somewhere and ...' He went on hurriedly, prompted by the ominous silence. 'She's utterly professional, Chris. I can vouch for her, Chris. She won't give you any trouble ...'

'Forget it, Paul.' Chris cut him short. 'You can cancel the interview. I thought I made it perfectly plain after the episode with that last "typist" you sent me that I won't have another hysterical beauty using typewritten pages instead of the proverbial bed sheets to creep into my life.'

'She isn't that sort, Chris!' The agent was genuinely angry now. 'She has been working with several of my writers and the only complaint I ever heard was that she was extremely uncooperative outside working hours. I just won't have you talk about her in that manner.'

Chris Donahue studied his agent's angry countenance, his well-shaped, firm mouth twisted into a crooked smile which hinted at the man's natural charm. 'Do I detect a chink in that old granite heart of yours?'

Paul Andrews didn't smile back. He liked Chris Donahue and admired him deeply but at times he found the man's hostile, contemptuous attitude to women hard to take. Not that it was an unjustified male arrogance. Even without his millions and his fame, the man was devastatingly attractive and naturally considered a most coveted prize by every ambitious predatory beauty. Once he seemed quite happy to take advantage of this untiring assault on his confirmed bachelorhood, changing girls more often than he had his hair cut and good-naturedly taking what they had to offer, giving very little of himself. But ever since his return from that journey of his, he had been rejecting them with an indifference which bordered on contempt. 'I find that attitude of yours quite worrying at times, Chris,' the agent said quietly. 'Not every girl you meet harbours a secret scheme to trap you into marriage, or an affair, you know.'

'Not *every* girl, no . . .' Chris Donahue's crooked grin soothed the older man's ruffled feathers.

'Anyway, it's too late to cancel the appointment. She should be here any moment now. You'll just have to see her.'

'All right, Paul, I will see her. But as I said, she's the last one. And just to make sure you don't force any more interviews on me, I'm leaving next week for the Seychelles and will spend the next few months on my yacht. Incommunicado and alone!'

The agent sighed, resignedly. 'I suppose I'll be wasting my breath asking you to give the girl a chance.' A curt nod confirmed his assumption. 'Oh, well, she'll survive, I guess. Ariel Stewart is a very resilient girl.'

'Ariel Stewart?' the writer's voice rose threateningly. 'Isn't she the one you have been trying to thrust on me ever since I came to you with my book?'

'Have I really been doing that?' Paul Andrews stopped at the door and turned an innocent face on his inquisitor. 'Perhaps. I don't remember. She's been working with so many of my writers, you see.' And not waiting to hear the younger man's explosive reaction, he hurriedly left the room, slamming the door shut after him.

Ariel Stewart was hopelessly late, as usual. Even today, facing the most important interview of her life, she couldn't manage to be on time. Somehow, though, she didn't think that would be too much of a set-back with the writer. He was far more likely to judge her potential usefulness by her wit and intelligence rather than her punctuality.

Paul Andrews, looking harassed and extremely agitated, was leaning against his black Jaguar. 'Good Lord, Ariel,' he called out, as her slim, long-legged body emerged out of the small Renault. 'You're even more exasperating than Chris Donahue. Do you realise I've been waiting down here for you for over half an hour?'

'Sorry, Paul.' The girl's lovely elfin eyes crinkled in a smile. 'I can't help it. I did try, honestly.'

The agent suppressed an involuntary smile. There was something about Ariel's natural, sprightly charm and good humour which made her irresistible even to cynical old horses like himself. 'Never mind now,' he said roughly. 'Let me look at you.'

His experienced eyes ran quickly over the girl's slender, tallish silhouette, noting the deceptively severe cut of the Armani suit which stressed rather than flaunted her feminine fragility. She seemed to have taken great care to create an impression of cool subtle trendiness. Even the long, auburn, flowing hair had been cropped fashionably short, framing the somewhat impish features and stressing the transparent complexion and the sparkling depth of the large, almond-shaped eyes. Anyone who had known her when she first came to London, some three years previously, would have found it hard to associate the beach-combing waif from the Seychelles Islands with this immaculate Sloane Ranger image.

'You'll do,' Paul Andrews conceded ungraciously. 'Slightly over the top, but you could be mistaken for a top executive secretary. Just remember to behave like one. He's expecting an efficient, unimaginative technician. Whatever you do, don't let him suspect that you're a script-writer.'

'Yes, I know. We've been over that dozens of times, Paul. You can trust me.'

The agent nodded. If anyone could carry out a convincing deception it would be Ariel Stewart. The girl's rich imagination was always ready to come up with ingenious details which made the most implausible story utterly believable. 'Listen, darling.' He concentrated now on cramming his young accomplice with as much information as he could. 'He's agreed to see you but that doesn't mean we've got him yet. I know you can turn most of us men around your little finger but don't underestimate him. He can see through people like a laser, Chris can. You'll have to use everything you've got to land the job.'

'I'll get it, Paul,' she assured the anxious agent, displaying a confidence which she certainly didn't feel.

'I wouldn't be too sure, darling. He's a hard case.' He studied the girl's guileless face thoughtfully, torn between affection and puzzlement. The girl had been pleading with him for months to get her a job, any job, with Chris Donahue, regardless of her growing success as a script-writer in her own right. For all he knew, the man was a total stranger to her and yet she seemed almost obsessed by a determination to get near him. But knowing the girl's baffling indifference to men, he was certain it was not a simple case of infatuation. 'Hang me if I understand why you want to do it, Ariel,' he said. 'It's such a giant step back for you. It'll mean cancelling your contract with Globe TV and you'll probably lose several other script commissions. I wish you would tell me why you're so keen on working with Chris Donahue.'

She turned away from his close scrutiny. 'I will, Paul. One day,' she promised and briskly walked to the gates to ring the intercom bell before he could pursue the subject further. The metallic sound of a female voice wafted through, asking for identification, and then instructed her to come on in. She was expected.

'I'll call you later, Paul,' she called out as the gate slid open to let her in. 'And thanks for getting me this interview.'

Paul Andrews watched her disappear beyond the gates and then turned away, sighing.

He had become her agent soon after her arrival in England having read some of her short stories. His literary agency, one of the oldest and most respectable in England, was not in the habit of taking on young, inexperienced writers, but he couldn't ignore the promise of her talent nor resist her warm, trusting charm. So he helped her break into the enclosed, tough world of film and TV and proudly watched her make a success of it. Over the years he had come to love her as a daughter but as such she had become a source of perpetual bewildered concern. For all her friendly, irresistible charm, there was something oddly secretive about her. She would happily chat about herself, her ambitions and her work, yet she hardly ever mentioned her life before she settled in England. All he managed to learn from her was that she came from an obscure little island in the Seychelles where her family had been settled for many generations. She spoke with amused affection of her strict, almost Victorian upbringing, of her colonial family, an almost extinct species of the old Empire days, but firmly refused to explain why she had left what she affectionately kept referring to as 'her island'.

'I wanted to write scripts,' was the only reason she gave him when he asked her. 'Besides, Michael needed someone to keep house for him.'

Michael was her older brother, a successful psychiatrist, who like her had decided to make a career in England, and with whom she shared the large Victorian house in Dulwich. Except for him, she seemed to be all alone in England and Paul couldn't help feeling that she was a fish out of water away from the sandy, sun-drenched beaches of her island. There was a sense of a caged bird about her, as if her natural bubbling joy of life was held by a leash. She seemed to be living on the fringe of life, waiting or looking for something or someone, and refusing to live fully until she found it. Well, he sighed softly as he stepped into his car. It seemed as if she had found it in Chris Donahue.

Oblivious of her agent's speculation, Ariel was hurrying along the path, her heart pounding painfully against her ribs as she approached the house.

It was as unconventional and striking as its owner: a clean-lined, ultra-modern white villa, the kind one would expect to find in very exclusive sunny resorts, certainly not against the very English country-like backdrop of Hampstead Heath. Yet, even in her panicked state, Ariel couldn't help wondering at how curiously well it merged with the lush landscape.

The wide oak front door opened into a spacious, sparsely furnished hall and a young girl, her bright red hair framing a small freckled face in wild disarray, was there to greet her. Dressed in the studied slovenliness which was very much Ariel's usual style, she was a far cry from the iron-maid Ariel had expected, having heard the cold metallic voice over the intercom.

'Miss Stewart, right?' The redhead was grinning up at her, not expecting an answer and went on to inundate Ariel with a flood of friendly, totally uncalled for information. 'I'm standing in for Chris's receptionist. He doesn't have one, incidentally. Only old faithful Marjorie and she's out, shopping. That's the housekeeper, by the way. She's been with the family for ages.' Her light blue eyes were scanning Ariel with a disarming friendly curiosity. 'I adore your suit. Armani, isn't it? Can you afford it on a secretary's salary?' And before Ariel could think of a cool retort, she continued, disarmingly, 'Sorry, am I being insufferable?'

Ariel chuckled and assured her that she was. The girl answered with a satisfied giggle. 'I know. I'm incorrigible. I'm Daria, by the way. Chris's niece.

Well, step-niece, to be more precise, and not exactly a niece either. My mother is married to his cousin, Neville. I just call him uncle to tease him. Chris, that is. Not Neville. Come on, he's waiting for you. You're number four today.'

There was something elusively familiar about the girl which was at once endearing and exasperating. It took Ariel several seconds before it suddenly dawned on her: the red-headed chatter-box could have been herself at the age of nineteen. That was hardly three years ago but she seemed to have aged a century since those carefree days in her native island of St Patrick, she thought grimly.

'Do you like being a secretary?' the redhead wanted to know.

'I guess I do,' Ariel lied coolly, 'otherwise I wouldn't be doing it, would I?'

She followed the girl into a vast living-room which seemed to occupy the space of a good-sized flat. The tasteful, unobtrusively expensive decor was given almost entirely to cool, natural tones except for the colourful paintings. It was obviously designed so that nothing would distract the eye from the breath-taking views of the Heath which sprawled beyond the huge, all-glass wall.

To her relief, the room seemed empty, and Daria's incessant chatter which hardly required any response from her was oddly soothing, allowing her time to collect her wits and calm her taut nerves. 'I could never be a secretary.' The girl was still harping on the same subject. 'I think I'd hate it. I mean, being cooped up in an office all day long, taking orders . . . I'd be hopelessly bad at it, anyway. Wouldn't I, Chris?' she continued, without pausing for breath.

Ariel turned around, in sudden panic. As far as she could see, there was no one else in that enormous room.

'*Uncle Chris*,' Daria raised her voice slightly, putting a mocking stress to the avuncular title. 'Don't skulk there. Come and meet her. She looks terribly sophisticated but I think she's very sweet. You'll adore her.'

'That's enough, Daria.' Ariel caught her breath as Chris Donahue's attractive voice came floating in from nowhere. 'Now get out of here and don't come back unless you bring some coffee with you.'

After a second of confusion, Ariel identified the direction of that mellow, lazy voice as coming from the paved patio which she could now see beyond the glazed wall.

He was wearing shabby fawn-coloured jeans and an outsize, flamboyant Montana jumper. The casual elegance of the seasoned jet-setter clashed with, yet curiously enhanced the strong clean lines of the hard face, the unruly thick mane of tawny, sun-bleached hair, and the weather-beaten complexion which spoke of a man who preferred the freedom and challenge of the outdoor life to the pampered existence of the idle rich.

Tall and long-legged, he was leaning with a typically athletic grace against the white-painted trellis, studying her calmly. His uncompromising expression showed neither hostility nor any sign of recognition.

'You will have a cup with me, won't you?' she heard him say, arrogantly refusing to defeat the distance between them by raising his voice.

The casual greeting she had prepared stuck in her throat. All she could muster was a weak, nervous smile.

'Am I to interpret that silence as a marked dislike for coffee?' he said after a short pause as he detached himself from the supporting trellis and walked back into the lounge with a carelessly graceful stride. 'Or would you prefer tea, perhaps? Or, better still, would you rather join me in something stronger?' he pursued, waving a tumbler of undiluted Scotch in her face, mockingly aware of her tongue-tied condition.

'Come on, Chris.' Daria came to her help. 'Can't you see you're intimidating the girl?' She turned to Ariel, smiling at her reassuringly. 'Don't let him bully you. He's only trying to frighten you off. The truth is that he'd rather not have anyone. You would like coffee, Miss Stewart, wouldn't you?'

The patronising attitude of the well-meaning girl shook Ariel out of her momentary awkwardness. 'I'd love some, thank you,' she said calmly, and the girl darted out of the room, promising it wouldn't take her a minute.

Ariel turned back to the man, and waited for him to make the first move. It was always the best strategy with arrogant bullies of his sort, she had found out.

Well, Chris Donahue could play the game just as well as she could. Polite and overtly bored, he just stood there, relaxed and loose-limbed, his deep blue eyes travelling indifferently over her body.

'May I sit down?' she blurted, almost rudely, when she could no longer stand that cool, assessing look.

'Oh yes, you certainly may. I've had enough time to admire your very impressive outfit. You didn't really think that I wouldn't recognise you in that new guise, did you?'

Fortunately, she was already seated when he uttered the last words, otherwise she would have collapsed. Her startled eyes met his as she began to stammer: 'Re-recognise me?'

'In case you have forgotten,' he said softly, mocking her. 'We have been introduced before. A couple of weeks ago, at the Mayfair Restaurant. Except that on that occasion you didn't look like a very upmarket Sloane Street commercial. More like a dishevelled street-urchin. Is that why you refused Paul Andrews's invitation to join us for lunch?'

Her rigid body sagged slightly in a confusion of relief and heart-piercing disappointment. As a matter of fact she had seen him several times over the last few months, making a point of turning up wherever he had been expected, but then, as now, she always encountered the same blank look of a total stranger. She was nothing to him but another pretty face. 'I'm sorry, Mr Donahue. I didn't think you'd remember me,' she said tightly. 'And just for the record, I didn't try to come here under a guise. I was just trying to create a good first impression ... I mean, second impression.'

If she hoped to break the ice by her easy banter, she soon had to admit defeat. He listened to her, his face shut, his eyes expressionless, making no effort to ease the first moments of the interview. Desperately, she had to go on chatting. 'I mean, I thought I'd better dress the part. I am supposed to apply for a job as a . . . a secretary, after all.'

'Are you now?' Again she tried to read a hidden meaning behind his lazy enquiry. His face revealed nothing.

'Of course I am. Didn't Paul Andrews explain?'

'Oh yes, he certainly did. According to the old man, he's entrusting me with his most cherished possession: a production secretary who is *au fait* with all the well-hidden secrets of script-writing and highly intelligent and experienced to boot. Are you?'

'Yes.' It was gratifying to see some response registered on that handsome, bored face. He was obviously taken aback by her unabashedly arrogant, short reply.

'Well, you're certainly not short of confidence.'

'I know what I'm good at, Mr Donahue.' The words were hardly out of her mouth before she realised that he could read a double meaning into them. She blushed, furious with herself. That impulsive tongue of hers always landed her in the most embarrassing traps. Her position was weak enough without offering Chris Donahue further ammunition to taunt her with. She forced her eyes to stare back at him, defiantly.

To her surprise, he didn't respond to the unintended challenge. 'Your name, I take it, is Ariel?' he asked, casually.

She took a deep breath, preparing herself for the next hurdle. 'Ariel Stewart,' she said.

'Like *The Tempest* Ariel?' She nodded. 'Unusual name,' he said after a short pause. 'But I'll settle for it. Well, good morning, Ariel.'

And then, unpredictably, he smiled.

Her heart leaped to her throat as the smile transformed the closed, uncompromising face, lighting up the watchful eyes and softening the ragged, handsome features to reveal humour, generosity and warmth. Trapped by its deceptive charm, Ariel responded with a radiant guileless smile of her own which very rarely failed to win her instant affection.

It was the wrong tactic. As if resenting his momentary lapse, his smile tightened slightly and his voice resumed a cooler, practical shade. 'I don't go for office hours. I'll expect you to work at the oddest times which may mean moving in with me. Perhaps even go away from London. You'll be out of circulation for three months at least. Can you take it?'

'I can if you can,' she answered, hardly daring to believe her ears. The job, it seemed, was hers before the battle had even started. 'Just tell me where, when and what.'

'How about why?' he broke in.

'Oh, I know why. For some odd reason, you want to adapt your novel yourself.'

'Is that so unusual?'

'Well, yes.' Ariel was off in the familiar world of her professional life. 'Most novelists prefer to plunge into their next novel instead of ploughing over the old one. Unless they need the money, which you obviously don't. You're a rare exception. I wonder why.'

'So there *is* a "why", after all.' His voice was soft, but Ariel, still glorying in her easy victory, was deaf to the warning bell.

'All right, then,' she plunged in. 'There is. But I wouldn't presume for a moment that you're ready to trust me with it.'

'How perceptive,' he congratulated her. 'So you don't mind being cooped up with me for several months? I warn you, it'll be only the two of us till we're finished. I work—*and* live, in total seclusion.'

'Of course,' she responded coolly, refusing to be baited by the deliberately coarse insinuation behind his last words. 'Where do you usually find it?'

'Here, among other places ... when I'm not invaded by my family. It'll be your job to keep them off my back.'

'Oh, but——' She spoke out unthinking and stopped. 'I mean, yes of course.'

He was too quick for her. 'What were you going to say, Ariel?'

It was useless denying her unguarded reaction: 'I thought ... That is, Paul Andrews said you might want to work on your yacht.'

'Would you like that?' he asked, the irony in his voice branding her as the sort of person who would be impressed by such jet-setting symbols.

'Oh, very much.' She kept her own voice sweet and innocent. 'I love the sea and I've been sailing our yacht ever since I can remember but I haven't had a chance to do so for three years now so naturally the idea appeals to me.'

'I see.' He grinned, acknowledging her subtle way of telling him that, like him, she was quite used to such luxuries. 'If that's the case, don't you think you ought to leave the job to someone who obviously needs the money more than you do?'

'No, I don't.' She bristled. It was the same old, trite argument against the bored little rich girl which she had had to contend with all her life. 'I would only leave it to someone who can do the job better. When do you want me to start?' She firmly put in her question before he could pursue the subject any further.

He didn't persist. 'How long will it take you to untangle yourself out of your other commitments?' He answered with a question.

Without thinking she answered: 'I've already done that. I'm free to start whenever you wish.'

He was silent for a moment, his eyes once more shut in a cool, speculative look. 'You were that sure you'd get the job?'

'Well, I was right, wasn't I?' she chuckled, still unsuspecting.

'Were you now?' Something in his voice wiped the easy smile off her lips. Her eyes rose to scan his face and suddenly she was reminded of Paul Andrews's warning: Chris Donahue could certainly see through people like a laser beam.

You little fool, she scolded herself furiously. The man had been toying with her all along, testing her, pretending to be taken in by her charm. She had been had!

'You mean, you don't want me?' she blurted, too mortified to notice the double meaning which could be applied to her question.

'I suppose that's exactly what I mean.'

She tried to control the quaver of deep disappointment. 'You haven't even bothered to ask about my qualifications, my experience . . .'

'Oh, I don't doubt those for a second. You're good. I'm quite happy to take your word for it,' he reassured her pleasantly. 'The trouble is that I don't trust you.'

'May I . . . may I know why?'

'Certainly,' Chris Donahue answered, readily. 'Because you're a schemer, and not a very subtle one at that. You would have applied for any old job, even if I advertised for a chambermaid. I don't know nor do I care to know what you were hoping to gain by it, but I do know one thing, darling.' His voice was light and pleasant, and the smile still devastatingly charming. Only the dark blue eyes mocked her coldly, as he concluded, relentlessly: 'It's not the job you're after. It's me.'

The words echoed in cold, lazy contempt through the vast room.

Ariel surfaced out of her momentary freeze to find that she was up on her feet. Humiliation and a helpless fury deadened all other feelings. Whatever he might have meant to her in the past, she now felt nothing but loathing for that conceited, suspicious stranger who was facing her with that bored, disdainful smile.

'Even if you were right, Mr Donahue,' her voice was tight with dislike, 'this interview has certainly changed my mind. Sorry for having taken so much of your time. Goodbye.'

As if taking her final word as a cue, the door swung open, and Daria marched in with a coffee tray. 'I hope it's all right,' she announced cheerfully, totally impervious to the strained atmosphere in the room. 'I used your new coffee-maker but I might have put too much coffee in. I brought hot water to thin it down if it's too strong.'

She practically pushed Ariel's rigid body back on to the sofa and thrust a cup of coffee into her hand and insisted she tasted it. Then, having taken a sip from her step-uncle's cup to check the result for herself, she now flopped happily on the sofa beside Ariel, clearly intending to join in on the interview.

'Well, is she in?' she attacked her uncle and immediately turned on Ariel, ignoring her furious silence. 'Have you discussed salary yet? You mustn't be modest, you know. Chris is disgustingly generous, so he deserves to be exploited. Don't worry, though. He'll make you earn every penny of it, believe me.'

The girl was either incredibly insensitive or a very clever manipulator but she had somehow managed to break through Ariel's debilitating rage and tickle her sense of humour. It was almost as if her younger self, that carefree, slightly dizzy tropical island waif, came back to revive her confidence in herself. She no longer cared whether she got the job or not. But she was damned if she would let this disagreeable bully of a writer chase her away with her tail between her legs.

'And you will let me try on that thing you're wearing, won't you? I think we're the same size,' Daria was chirping on, blithely. 'My mother keeps insisting on buying me the most ridiculously boring clothes but I'm sure I'd be a knock-out in that.'

'Cut it out, Daria!' Chris Donahue barked.

'Haven't you finished yet?' the girl asked, pouting. 'You've been grilling the poor girl for over fifteen minutes now.'

'That's none of your business,' her step-uncle answered drily. 'Don't try to be cute now, Daria!'

'Oh, come off it, *Uncle* Chris——'

'Get out!' he exploded at last.

In deep admiration Ariel watched the laughing eyes brim with instant tears and the impish face crumple into a clown mask of utter dejection, as the red-headed brat stood up and made her slow, despondent retreat to the door. The girl had a brilliant comic talent and

Ariel couldn't hold back her mirth, hard as she tried to keep a solemn face.

Her breathless silvery laughter rippled through the still room, drawing two startled pairs of eyes in her direction.

Daria stopped and turned around. For a moment she gaped open-mouthed at the cool, elegant woman who had been transformed by that wonderful, irrepressible laughter into someone as young and dizzy as herself; and then, she joined in. It took both girls several seconds before it dawned on them that they had exactly the same laughter: breathless, silvery, and quite enchanting.

They stopped laughing and stared at each other in stunned incredulity and then, struck by the odd coincidence of their similar laughter, they gave way to a renewed wave of spontaneous, uncontrollable giggles.

Chris Donahue was forgotten. Neither girl was aware of the haunted expression which darkened the hard, lean face, and the troubled look in the blue-black eyes which kept roving, unblinking, from one laughing girl to the other. Suddenly, as if tormented beyond endurance by the silver sound, he stood up abruptly and walked out through the French doors into the large patio outside.

The laughter died on Daria's face, instantly replaced by a deeply troubled look which revealed the sensitivity and depth behind the frivolous façade. Silently, she threw Ariel a warning glance and tip-toed out of the room.

Ariel remained seated, her dark eyes deep with understanding and pain fixed on the tall, rigid figure out on the patio. He looked so alone, so far away . . . utterly lost. Her heart went out to him but she knew better than to offer sympathy or help to that proud man. She waited a few minutes and then poured fresh coffee into his cup and joined him outside.

'Your coffee.' She put it on the small patio table, her voice cool and matter-of-fact. 'It was getting cold.' He didn't seem to hear her.

The chilly wind was ruffling her short hair as she

waited, staring out into the early spring landscape of the Heath to avoid the look of naked torment which darkened the handsome face.

His voice was calm and low when he spoke again. 'Do you live in London?'

'I do now,' she answered, still not daring to look at him. 'I came here three years ago.'

'Where from?'

'From the Seychelles Islands,' she said tightly. 'St Patrick.'

'I know the Seychelles quite well but I don't think I've ever been to your particular island.'

'It's very small, practically uninhabited,' she began to explain, but his intent blue eyes, narrowly focused on her pale, unguarded face, robbed her of words.

They stared at each other, their bodies far apart, yet their eyes locked as if in a physical contact. For once, there were no shields of polite coolness, no defences of mockery or dislike. They were stripped open to each other, unafraid to expose their vulnerability.

'Ariel ...' he mumbled, as if to himself. 'Ariel Stewart, is that right?'

She nodded, holding her breath. For an endless moment he seemed to be struggling with his memory, trying to make a connection. But finally he shook his head. She knew he was seething with angry frustration.

'I ... I'd better be going now,' she said softly, when the silence threatened to tear her nerves to shreds.

'Wait!' His voice was louder, slightly menacing. 'I have one more question to ask you.'

Ariel stopped, one foot over the threshold of the lounge. 'Turn around,' he ordered and then softened his harsh command with a grudging 'please.' She obeyed, but kept her eyes down.

He didn't speak for a long moment. 'We've known each other before, haven't we.' It wasn't a question. He was stating a fact. 'And I don't mean those hit-and-run encounters you've been staging around London either, so don't try to be funny. I know I've heard your laughter before.'

She carefully chose her words so that she wouldn't be lying outright. 'Of course you have. It's exactly like Daria's. We were both amazed by the similarity.'

'Yes, quite, but that's not what I meant,' he said absently. 'I had the same feeling when I heard Daria laugh. That's why I have such a soft spot for her, I suppose.' He shook his head, as if impatient with himself for lapsing into that unguarded confession. 'Just tell me. Have we met before?'

'I . . . I don't think so.' She was trembling inside but her voice came out light and impersonal. 'You must be confusing me with someone else.'

She suffered his long, careful scrutiny unflinchingly. Then she could breathe freely again as his stern mouth softened in a grin. 'My mistake, then. And the job is yours, if you still want it.'

There was no sense of glowing triumph, no relief. Only an instant awareness that her troubles were only just beginning.

'I do,' she said when she could trust her voice. 'Thank you.'

'Don't mention it,' he mumbled drily. 'I'm willing to give it a trial run but don't get me wrong. I still don't trust you.'

Left raw and vulnerable by those few unexpected minutes of close contact, she almost reeled under the candid cruelty of his statement. 'I understand,' she said tightly. 'When . . . when do you want me to start?'

'Tomorrow morning,' he said shortly, throwing the words over his shoulder as he strode back towards the spacious lounge, forcing her to hurry after him. 'We'll give it a go for a few days, before we make a final decision. Meanwhile, I suggest you move in here. As I said, I don't stick to normal working hours and I'd rather you didn't drive home alone late at night.' Abruptly, he turned around and gave her an impersonal, cool look. 'Marjorie, my housekeeper, lives here permanently, in case you were wondering.' He was perfectly civil but the dry voice assured her that her virtue was the last thing he was interested in. 'Is that all right with you?'

Again she nodded, trying to match his cool impersonal manner. 'Would you mind if I brought my word-processor? It's portable and I write ... I mean, I type much faster with it.'

'Don't bother.' He smiled mechanically. 'You can use mine. It's in the study. Ask Daria or Marjorie to show you around. Is there anything else you'd like to know?'

She shook her head, aware of his obvious impatience to bring the interview to an end. He was standing by the oak door which led into the hall, blocking her exit, one hand on the brass knob. 'I'll ... I'll see you tomorrow,' she stammered, wondering how she would manage to squeeze past him on her way out.

She bent down to collect her shoulder bag and the heavy unbound manuscript, his steady gaze making her feel clumsy and uneasy.

'Ariel ...' She stopped dead as the sound of her name engulfed her like a physical caress. 'Yes?' she said, turning her eyes on him.

He went on in the same warm, low voice. 'There's one thing I'd better mention before we start. Since we're going to be living in each other's pocket, I suppose I'll have to let you in on the secret. The family skeleton, so to speak. You're bound to hear about it from Daria or from some other member of my loving family, so you might as well get it from me. I won't insult you by suggesting that you keep it to yourself.'

Her heart was pounding so loudly that she was sure he could hear it.

'You have heard about my disappearing act some three years ago?'

Ariel nodded. 'I ... I read about it.'

'Yes, I thought you had. Well, wouldn't you like to know what happened to me during those unaccounted-for six months in my life?'

'Yes.' Ariel's voice was hardly a whisper.

'It's quite simple, my dear,' he went on, his voice dry and colourless. 'The truth is, I don't know myself. You see, I have lost my memory.'

His voice sounded so casual, so matter-of-fact, as if he was talking about a slight headache, yet Ariel was well aware of the inner turmoil, the effort it had taken him to say these words out loud.

She didn't attempt to break the long silence. At last, she raised her eyes to meet his, directly.

Chris smiled. 'You don't look surprised, or shocked. Maybe you didn't understand me properly. There's a black hole in my life ... a six-months' blank. Six months in which I lived as another person, and I haven't got the foggiest idea of where, how or who I was. What's more,' he continued softly, menacingly, 'I don't know what I have been up to during those months. For all I know I could have killed, robbed, raped or——'

'Or just wandered about, lost and confused but probably just as sane as you are now,' she finished, almost vehemently.

Her forceful interruption startled him. She gave him a slight, apologetic smile. 'My brother is a psychiatrist,' she explained. 'So I've heard of such cases before. I seem to remember him saying that, like in a hypnotic state, a man who suffers from temporary amnesia rarely acts against his basic nature.'

'Only rarely?' he mocked her gently. 'So there are a few exceptions to the rule, nevertheless.'

'I suppose there are, but somehow I don't think you are one of them. And you don't believe it either, Mr Donahue,' she finished, almost angrily.

The handsome face broke into a wide grin and for the first time she had heard him laugh out loud: 'All right, then. And my name is Chris, by the way.' He offered his hand, in a gesture of mock formal introduction. Ariel hesitated, but finally let him take her hand in a strong, warm grasp.

'We'll assume then that I'm no psychotic killer or rapist.' He grinned down at her. 'But you will find me moody, unpredictable and unreasonable. And you'd better not ask me questions at such times or try to be sympathetic. I can be quite temperamental when something touches a raw nerve. Like when——'

'Like when you heard me laughing.' She didn't mean to say that, but the words just came out.

The silence that followed terrified her. She stole a look through her lashes, expecting an exasperated rebuke at her uncalled-for intervention. Instead, he just looked down at her, with a curiously warm smile in his eyes. Yet she knew it wasn't her he was seeing but someone else. Someone without a face or a body . . . a ghost.

'Yes,' he said softly, almost to himself. 'Like when I heard you laughing. I'm sure I've heard that laughter before, but it belongs in another place . . . somewhere warm and humid, where the sea is slow and lazy and the horizon is always misty . . . Just sounds, smells, texture, that wonderful, breathless laughter and . . .' His distant gaze came down to fasten, as if in a question, on the palms of his hands. 'And my hands buried in long, flowing, sun-warmed hair. . .

His eyes strayed towards her own short-cropped hair and then saw her large dark eyes, glinting with unshed tears. 'Oh, for Heaven's sake! Don't look at me with those big, unhappy eyes!' His tone was dry and impatient again but almost instantly it softened again, thinking he had terrified her by letting her have a glimpse of the gaping black hole which tormented him. 'Sorry, darling. It's only my blasted memory playing hide-and-seek with me again. Don't let it upset you.'

She nodded dumbly.

'Come on, Ariel. I want to hear you laugh again.'

She swallowed, her lips too rigid to respond even with a smile. 'I can't. I'm sorry.'

He looked at her for a second, trying to dispel her fear with his warm, friendly smile, and then, as if losing interest or patience, he turned away and in his graceful loose-limbed stride, left the room.

CHAPTER TWO

I WANT to hear you laugh again . . .

The same voice, the same warm smile, the same intimate command . . . as if the cold marble shell of the writer had cracked open to let through the man she had lost three long years ago.

'Oh, Kane!'

The room echoed with the sound of his old name and she looked around in panic, in case her unguarded moan was heard by anyone. But there was no one there and she sank into the deep armchair in which he had sat before, finding some comfort in the imagined warmth of his body.

Kane . . .

She gave him that name when he had told her, his voice dull with horror, that he had none. She wasn't sure why she had pounced on that specific name. But hard and unyielding, it reflected something of the man who had been banished from his past by the loss of his memory and stumbled onto her island and into her life. A Creole fisherman had found his unconscious body on the beach and carried him to the shelter of his nearby shack. There was no sign of a yacht or even a sailing boat, so it was assumed that he had swum over from one of the larger islands, had collapsed mid-way and had been washed ashore. He was in a coma for two days before the Creole's wife, who happened to be the Stewart children's old nanny, noticed the alarming swelling of the bruise at the back of his head and decided to confide in her old charges. The man needed medical care and luckily Dr Mike, Ariel's older brother, was home from England, on his Christmas holiday.

Michael wasn't exactly enthralled by the prospect of getting involved with this particular case. The kindly Creole couple had found no passport, no cards, nothing in fact which could identify the unconscious man, and Michael's first thought was that he could be a political or criminal fugitive. St Patrick had been often used as a haven for such people: it was scantily inhabited and mostly by Creoles, the Stewarts being the only European family. And being politically insignificant, it had no police, no government representatives and no tourist facilities whatsoever. As such, the island offered a perfect temporary hide-out for wanted men.

Nevertheless, being a doctor, Michael could hardly refuse to see a sick man no matter how suspicious the circumstances, and Ariel, who could never resist her insatiable curiosity, insisted on coming with him.

That's how Kane invaded her life.

She was nineteen years old and just back from six long years of boarding school in England. Her parents felt she should go back to England, perhaps take a university degree, but she kept putting it off. She loved her island passionately and had missed it terribly while away at school. She had been back a year now, and she was still enchanted by its primeval beauty and the slow, peaceful pace of the uneventful days. The outside world meant a relentless rat-race of the competitive challenges which she was in no hurry to join. As for social life, she found all the fun and companionship she needed among the many friends she had on the larger islands, and careerwise, she had long ago decided on writing, and her stories were already being published regularly in England, so there was no need for her to pursue her career away from St Patrick.

Love . . . well, that was another matter. She wanted it, fantasised about it, wrote about it endlessly in her stories, but never came across it until she met Kane.

He was lying on the rush bed, in the sparse Creole shack, his deathly pale face hardly discernible behind several days' growth of beard, which like the overgrown dark blond hair was dull and sticky with sea-water. His eyes were shut, and his lean body, naked under the threadbare blanket, was alarmingly still.

'He's dead, Michael, isn't he?' Ariel turned her

eyes away in sick horror.

Michael, with four years' hospital practice behind him, coolly ordered her out of the house if she was going to be a nuisance. 'He isn't dead, you twit. Badly concussed, though. No bones broken, as far as I can judge, and no signs of exposure. He must be as tough as doornails to have survived that nasty head blow and God knows how many hours at sea.'

It might have been the sound of an English voice, or just plain coincidence, but the heavy eyelids fluttered and suddenly his eyes were open and he was staring straight into hers.

Even in the dim light of the single naked bulb, the dark-blue gaze shone with piercing brilliance, deep and unguarded, too hazy to erect any barriers between them. He was welcoming her not as a stranger but as a trustworthy friend. She smiled at him and her heart leaped to her throat when he responded with a weak grin. Later she confessed that she fell in love with him at that very moment.

'Do you speak English?' Michael asked cautiously, unaware of the mute but shattering exchange between his sister and his patient.

The man could only give a weak nod and tried to sit up. Michael laid a restraining hand on his shoulder: 'Lie down. And don't try to talk. You've been unconscious for several days, and not having any facilities here, I can't judge how bad your condition is. I might have to move you to the main hospital on Mahe.'

There was another weak nod and the eyes seemed to transmit meek acceptance. She could see no sign of fear or anxiety.

'Michael is a doctor.' She hurriedly fell into an elaborate explanation, afraid he might go to sleep again and she would lose the contact with those wonderful deep blue eyes. 'He's my brother, by the way and my name is Ariel. Like Ariel in *The Tempest*. Do you know it?' He nodded weakly, mouthing the word 'Shakespeare'.

'Shut up, Ariel.' Michael decided his patient had had enough for now. 'There's nothing more I can do right now. We'll wait till tomorrow and see how you're getting along. Sleep, hopefully, will do the trick. I'll be back in the morning.'

'Hey, wait a minute, Mike. You're not thinking of leaving him here?' Ariel interrupted with her customary impulsiveness. 'We're moving him to the house.'

'Oh no, we're not!' Michael cut her short. 'Leaving aside the fact that he can't be moved anywhere in his condition, I also don't think Dad will be overjoyed by the prospect of harbouring a wanted man.'

'He isn't, Mike.' She didn't bother to lower her voice. 'He didn't seem at all anxious when you spoke of moving him to the main island. Which he would have been if he were a fugitive.' The humorous glint which lit up the dark blue gaze was her reward for her impulsive trust.

She was there again the next day, and the day after. In fact, she hardly left her old nanny's shack. She was a hopeless nurse but fortunately, he needed very little nursing. He just slept, seeming to grow stronger in staggering stages. Michael no longer talked of moving him to a hospital.

Three days went by before he became fully awake and could speak to her. His first words were unpredictable, almost whimsical. Later on she became utterly fascinated by his habit of coming up with the most unexpected but oddly perceptive remarks. She was sitting cross-legged on the floor beside his makeshift bed, devouring a huge slice of mango and getting her face all smeared with the juice, when his voice made her jump out of her skin.

'So they do eat after all.' His low, attractive voice reached down to her and if she hadn't been already infatuated, that wonderful caressing voice would have done the trick. 'And I always thought that spirits were above such things as food.'

'Of course they are,' she answered, recovering from her momentary shock. 'And I'm not a spirit.'

'So it isn't really enchanted then?' he asked.

She knew immediately what he was referring to, as if their minds were tuned together. 'Our island? Not really. But my mother likes to think of it as Prospero island. That's why she called me Ariel.'

He nodded, his blue eyes glinting with amusement. 'Sure you're not a spirit?' he mumbled.

Ariel burst out laughing and saw his eyes widen momentarily with warm pleasure. 'No, certainly not a spirit. Too exasperatingly human, if you asked Michael or my father.'

He didn't need to ask more about the island or about herself, she had been feeding him with endless information for days now. In fact, having been discarded by her nanny as a nurse, she limited her usefulness to interminable and probably exasperating babble.

She still had no inkling of the man's real problem. Nor had he, to judge by his tranquil, untroubled blue gaze and his amused responses to her endless chirpy chatter. The truth burst on them all when Ariel suddenly remembered that they still didn't know his name.

It was then that she saw for the first time the bewildered, frantic look which dulled the sparkle of his deep blue gaze. 'I don't know,' he said after a long pause, and repeated as if to himself, 'God help me, I don't know . . .'

She could never forget those dreadful hours when the horror of his situation gradually dawned on him. He remembered absolutely nothing. His home, his parents, his occupation, not one single detail of his past. All they could tell was that he was English, somewhere in his early thirties and probably a public-school and Oxbridge man, going by his accent and his manners. That was about it. The rest was a terrifying blank vacuum in which he stumbled blindly. Desperately, helplessly lost. A man without a past!

When Michael was informed of the man's predicament, he took matters into his own hands. 'Look, friend,' he said practically. 'It's probably a temporary loss of memory. It can happen in bad cases of concussion. You won't help matters much by getting all tense and frantic about it. Give it time.'

'Kane,' Ariel blurted out of the blue, breaking into her brother's cool reasoning. 'I'll call you Kane.'

'Why?' Michael asked.

'I don't know. Its just seems to fit. Do you mind?' she turned to the newly baptised man.

Something in her unshakeable, infectious high spirits seemed to have broken through the shocked horror of his predicament. Chuckling with relief, she saw the cloudy eyes come to life, and the firm, tight mouth relax in the lazy grin which had already enslaved her. 'Why not?' he said. 'What's in a name, after all? I suppose I should be grateful to you for not baptising me Neville, or Nigel or Christopher.'

'Christopher . . .' She tried the name, several times. 'Actually, I rather like Christopher.'

'No, definitely not Christopher,' he stated bluntly, the smile gone.

Michael was watching him thoughtfully. 'It could be a name from your past, you know. Every free association like that is significant, so the more you talk the faster you'll regain your memory. There's nothing else you can do for now. Just live through it.' He smiled, no longer the doctor but her humorous, much loved brother again. 'You can thank your lucky stars, you know. You couldn't have asked to be stranded in a better place. St Patrick is just the place to lead a totally uneventful, sheltered, peaceful life.'

A week later, physically fit except for the recurring pangs of headache, and outwardly resigned to his temporary amnesia, Kane moved into their large plantation house. It was Michael's idea:

'If we sent you now to England, you'd probably be treated as a nut-case until you regained your memory. You're better off here, in St Patrick. No one here will bother you with questions, except my sister, that is. I'd keep away from her, if I were you. She's quite capable of driving you batty with her chatter.'

They introduced him to their parents as a friend of a friend of Michael's who had come from England to the Seychelles to recuperate after a long illness. And Ariel, her rich imagination working overtime, filled any possible gaps with an ingenious supply of background information.

Kane, according to Ariel's gospel, was a film script-writer. One of the reasons he had chosen to recuperate on St Patrick was a screenplay he had been working on and which happened to take place in an isolated island in the Indian Ocean.

'Why a script-writer?' Kane turned on her mildly when they were alone. 'Why not a novelist while you're at it?'

'Because my father is an avid reader and he would want to read one of your books. On the other hand, he's vehemently opposed to films and television. There isn't one on the island, anyway. So you're quite safe there.'

Kane accepted her reasoning. 'All right, but why make me a writer in the first place?'

'I don't know. It just felt right.'

He laughed. 'All right, then. Actually, I find the idea rather intriguing.'

Her mother, even her stiffly proper father, were quickly caught up in the spell of Kane's casual charm, manners and humour. 'Nice to know that England can still produce such young men,' her father remarked drily. 'I told you, Michael. The old system still works.'

There was no doubt that Kane had led quite a privileged life in the past. Putting aside his extensive knowledge and sophisticated taste, he also turned out to be magnificently adept at water-sports. Even in his weakened physical condition, he proved to be a great water-skier, skin-diver and long-distance swimmer, better than Ariel and Michael who were almost of professional standard. And he handled the Stewarts' yacht with an expertise that aroused Michael's good-natured envy.

After two weeks together, it was hard to remember the circumstances which had brought Kane into their life. He and Michael had become good friends, both treating her with the exasperated affection of older brothers. To all intents and purposes, they were all spending a vigorous and very enjoyable holiday together. Only those persistent if occasional twinges of sharp headaches kept reminding them of Kane's initial near-death condition.

But to Ariel's growing frustration, the fitter Kane became, the less she saw of him. He seemed perpetually drawn to the silent isolation of the island's forests and hills, or the vast blue desert of the Indian Ocean. When pestered, he would agree to join her in her various pastimes, but it was obvious to her that he preferred the loneliness of his own company to hers.

'Leave him alone, Ariel,' Michael exploded once, just before he left for England. 'Don't you see that he's going through hell? Try and imagine yourself waking up one fine day to find out that you are a stranger to yourself, that you have no past.'

As it happened, Ariel's fictitious profession for Kane proved to be an inspired flight of fantasy. The film justified Kane staying on after Michael returned to his hospital duties in London, and his writing gave Ariel a good excuse to spend time with him.

'Breakfast is ready!' she announced, bursting into his bedroom the morning after Michael's departure. 'Holiday's over. Get up, Kane!'

Kane, she had discovered, wasn't at his best in the mornings. He still needed long hours of sleep and, he once explained to her, whatever he might have been in his other life, he felt in his bones that he was never required to be up at the crack of dawn, which was Ariel's daily custom.

'Go away, Ariel!' he now mumbled sleepily, covering his head under the pillow to escape the bright morning light.

'Oh no you don't!' she insisted. 'You're getting up and coming with me to my beach shed. Your typewriter has just been delivered from Mahe.'

Kane groaned. 'What the hell are you talking about?' He sat up, the sheet slipping down to bare his lean, deeply tanned chest.

'Writing . . . that's what I'm talking about. You're a writer, remember? So you'd better do some writing. Just to keep my parents quiet.'

'And you just keep that skimpy bikini of yours out of my bedroom. I may have lost my memory, but my body still remembers what to do with a naked woman.'

Ariel blushed. She suddenly felt ridiculously awkward, like an adolescent schoolgirl. From the first moment she laid eyes on him, she never tried to deny or curb her infatuation, but not until this very minute was she consciously aware of the aching physical thrill his sight awakened in her.

'I always take a swim first thing in the morning,' she said defiantly. 'Don't expect me to change my dressing habits just because you're staying with us.'

'I wouldn't dream of it,' he assured her, his eyes roaming over her lithe, golden body, still shimmering with salty sea-water. 'As long as you stay away from me when I'm wearing even less.'

'Oh, don't be such a prude, Kane.' She tried to reverse their new disturbing roles back to the familiarly comfortable ones, where he was the weak recuperating patient, she the one in control.

Grinning at her indignant face, he rolled out of bed with a lazy animal grace, and walked to the door where she stood, utterly at ease and uninhibited by his nakedness. 'So who is the prude now, Ariel Stewart?' His low chuckle chased her as she escaped from the room in panic.

She covered herself up in one of Michael's huge T-shirts and tatty jeans which were cut at the knees, furious with herself for letting him intimidate her, anticipating his mocking acknowledgement of her unusually modest clothes.

The Stewarts' solidly built plantation house was situated a few hundred yards up the hill, almost hidden from view behind a screen of ancient tacamaca trees and tropical bushes. A long winding snake of narrow stone steps was the only convenient access down the steep slope to the white sandy beach and her improvised 'study'.

It was, in fact, just an open shed, covered by giant palm fans and supported by beams, giving her an uninterrupted view of the lazy, blue ocean and the small bay where the Stewarts' yacht, their only means of commuting with the main islands, was moored. Her book-loving father, secretly delighted with her choice of career, arranged to connect the primitive shed to the main house generator, so that she could work after nightfall and above all enjoy the luxury of an electric typewriter. The rest was spartan and sparse, only a few rocky chairs and two folding tables.

By the time Kane had joined her in her 'study' she felt in control again. She made him sit in front of the small manual typewriter which she had ordered from Victoria a few days earlier, deftly inserted a blank page, and ordered him to start writing. Then, prim and smug, she walked away to do the final revisions on her latest story, settling on her favourite rock, her feet dangling a few inches above the clear water of the gently rolling ocean.

To her own amazement, the familiar sound of a typewriter at work suddenly ruffled the still air. Slow and hesitant at first, it soon began to gather momentum, ending up in a furiously busy rattle.

She let him work alone for an hour, and then came softly to stand behind him. Her presence didn't seem to stop the flood.

'That's not a film script!' she couldn't help remarking after a few moments. 'That looks to me remarkably like the beginning of a novel.'

'I guess it is,' Kane agreed calmly. 'As much as I'd love to justify your inspired guess, I have no idea how to tackle a script. I don't think I've ever seen one. Sorry, Ma'am.'

She bent down, politely. 'May I read the first pages?'

'You may, teacher,' he answered, meekly, still typing away.

The first thing that struck her was his obvious familiarity with artificial intelligence and computing science.

'You seem to know a hell of a lot about computers,' she mumbled.

'Don't I?' he mumbled, typing away.

'Isn't it odd that you should remember nothing of your personal life, yet retain all that detailed information which you have obviously been accumulating through your studies and reading.'

He didn't answer. Obviously the thought had occurred to him too.

He had instinctively opted for the genre of Science Fiction . . . no, rather Science Fantasy, the kind which made books like *Dune* or films like *Close Encounters of the Third Kind* so popular. The period was the present, but the plot involved the meeting of three worlds, past, future and present, all clashing by a quirk of time-span on a small, hardly inhabited island in the Indian Ocean. The scientific fluency was amazingly well-matched with the hard, masculine prose and a fascinatingly rich plot which seemed to unfold almost from the first paragraph.

Totally unconscious of the voluptuous provocation of her gesture, Ariel threw her head back, scooping her long, chestnut hair to the top of her crown, and burst into her silvery breathless chuckle. 'Well, well, well,' she declared, smugly. 'So much for Dr Michael Stewart. All you need to bring your memory back, Kane, is having me around. I've obviously hit the nail right on the head when I made you a writer. You are, of course. I mean, you were in your other life.'

He usually reacted with indulgent good nature to all her wild assumptions about his past. But this time, he turned to her, his expression grave, thoughtful. 'I don't think so, Ariel. The moment I started writing, I felt as if something in me had been unleashed, set free from a long self-inflicted prison. I actually felt wicked, like a naughty boy secretly indulging in some forbidden game instead of doing his homework.' He smiled, crookedly. 'I think it means that I've always wanted to write, but never felt free to do so.'

Losing all interest in her own work, Ariel now flopped on the soft white sand, settling comfortably at Kane's bare feet, and proceeded to devour the typed pages as they came out of the small typewriter one by one at amazing speed. He didn't seem to mind her intrusion into his private creative world. In fact, he seemed oblivious of her existence. She felt a twinge of envy at the effortless ease in which he seemed to pick the right word, the exact turn of phrase first time round. His first draft hardly needed any revisions. Even his spelling was faultless, she commented sourly to herself.

The sun was beginning to set in red splendour over the misty horizon when she looked up, her eyes wide with the dawning realisation:

'Kane!' Her grave voice made him stop typing and look down to absorb her perplexed expression. 'What do you know about *The Tempest*?'

Without pausing to think, he answered lazily, as if humouring a child: 'Shakespeare, last play, Enchanted Island, such stuff as dreams are made on, Prospero, Miranda, Ariel ...' He stopped, in sudden awareness of what he was saying.

'You're basing your novel on *The Tempest*.' She confirmed his awakened suspicion.

They stared at each other, silently. And suddenly, Ariel burst out laughing, her radiant face trustingly open to his piercing blue eyes.

'I love your laugh.' He spoke so softly she wasn't sure she heard him. 'It's the one thing that makes this hell worthwhile.'

Bewildered by the painful, uncharacteristic heavy tone, she sat up, her laugh faltering.

'No, don't stop!' He bent down, his hands stretched out to take hold of her head between them, the long fingers spread to capture the sides of her small, impish face. 'Don't stop laughing.' His thumbs were stroking the wide forehead as if trying to smooth away the worried frown.

'I can't, Kane,' she apologised huskily, shaken by the warm grasp of his hands as much as by his confession. 'I ... I didn't realise you were so unhappy.'

Kane slid down from the chair to kneel on the soft sand, his head bowed down to study her face closely.

'I'm not. Not at this minute. You almost fill the

gaping hole of my life. So don't look so distressed. Come on, smile at me.' His finger touched the corner of her lips, jokingly trying to pull it into a smile.

'It must be awful,' she whispered, as her imagination, lulled by the sheltered life she had led until now, only now began to grasp the horror of living without a memory. 'Oh, Kane . . . I wish I could do something.'

He smiled down at her, but his eyes were dark with agony he couldn't hide. 'Just be there, that's enough . . . Oh, hell,' his voice dropped as he noticed the tears brimming her eyes, 'don't start crying, darling. That's no help at all, you know.'

'I'm sorry, I can't help it.'

With a groan, his hands came down on her sagging shoulders, and he scooped her into his arms, holding her head tight against his warm bare chest, comforting her as if it were she who was going through this hell, not he.

She had never felt so safe, so sheltered as she did now, cradled by his strong arms against that smooth hard chest, and soothed by the steady, strong beat of his heart.

Finally, she gave a shaken chuckle. 'I'm not crying any more,' she said as she raised her head, but her smile was arrested before it could form on her lips.

His face was only a few inches above her, illegible behind the blond beard. His masculine smell reached her flaring nostrils, and her eyes opened wide as they encountered the exposed hunger in his blue gaze.

She remained motionless, almost rigid in her breathless anticipation of what was coming, her wide-open eyes fixed unblinking on his bearded face as it came slowly down, soon to dissolve into a hazy blur. Then she had to shut her eyes and there was nothing but a tingling darkness as she felt the rasp of his beard on her cheeks and at last the touch of his mouth on her half-open, unknowing lips.

Neither had the will or the thought to stop the inevitable kiss, forgetting how exposed they were in the open shed. His hand was circling her long neck, luxuriating in the warm richness of the heavy hair, as his mouth barely opened to savour her lips in airy, light kisses, softly insistent, until she began to kiss him back, timidly.

His hold tightened, pulling her unresisting body closer to him, and at the same time bending her backwards until she could feel the soft warm sand under her bare skin, while his lips kept stirring her dormant senses to life with slow, deliberate insistence.

His arm slipped under her to encircle her narrow waist, rolling her on her side and gathering her to him as he stretched alongside her taut, still uncomprehending body, one hand slipping down to pull her hips against his own, moulding her form against his hard, long body, willing it to emerge out of its stunned rigidity, his warm hands whispering at her sleeping sensuality, urging it gently to respond, to take over, to rebel against the domination of the mind.

Something was happening to her, taking control over her nerveless muscles, melting them into total submission. She was sinking slowly into a dark sensual well, conscious only of the unrelenting, yet still gentle pull of the two hard hands, and the slow movement of the firm lips, open now to capture her whole mouth.

She had been kissed before, of course, and had always enjoyed the pleasant tingling thrill of those tentative embraces, but never before had she felt that torturing ache which made her whole body quiver with the terrifying need to get nearer, closer, push beyond the confining barriers of her loose T-shirt, even beyond the bare skin of his chest, to be wholly sucked into that hard wall of smooth, sinewy muscles.

Her arms, tentative and timid at first, rose to touch the warm, smooth texture of his bare back with escalating impatience, taunted by the unbearable torture of those slow, barely moving lips, her own mouth opened, hungry for more than that frustratingly teasing contact, and she moaned, utterly unprepared for the hard moist sweetness of his tongue as it thrust forward to take full possession of her mouth.

She felt an almost imperceptible shudder go

through his body as his warm hand moved between their tightly pressed bodies, pushing under the T-shirt to cup her breast, gently savouring its firm roundness, the long fingers toying, teasing. Then, tearing his mouth away from her demanding lips, his head came down to her exposed breasts, the grazing beard tormenting her skin, and with a barely audible groan his lips captured the aroused, erect tip making her whole body quiver as his flickering tongue set to torment her further with yet another new, unfamiliar thrill.

She was vaguely, frustratingly aware of confining bits of clothes, which kept her from losing all distinction as to where her body ended and his began. Their legs were intertwined now, one muscled thigh pushing hard between hers. Both his hands, voraciously, deliciously greedy, were roaming down her back, savouring the silky texture of her exposed skin, and finally struggling with the tight waist band of jeans to push further down and cover the firm mounds under it, cutting her breath as with one powerful jerk they pulled her against his flat stomach.

The lower part of her body recoiled as if scathed, startled by the strange, thrilling sensation of something vibrant stirring, growing, lashing out against her stomach. And she lay quiet, for a second, not quite comprehending, startled by the wonder of it.

She was now suddenly aware of a slight chill, a sense of physical bereftness, as if severed from what had become one with her own body. The sound of the calmly rolling sea, the swaying arms of the huge palm trees, penetrated the ethereal silence into which she had been plunged.

And Kane was sitting up, grinning down at her startled, crestfallen expression.

'Nineteen and never been kissed before,' he mocked lazily, but his eyes, still sparkling with hunger, were deep with warm tenderness. 'This really is an enchanted island.'

A burst of indignant exasperation covered her deep, trembling embarrassment. 'Don't be ridiculous, Kane.

Of course I've been kissed before.' During the first few days of his convalescence, she had entertained him with a blow-by-blow description of all her past adventures. It was quite an impressive list, she thought.

'Have you now?' His laughter mocked her gently.

'Oh, all right.' She laughed back, still shaky and breathless. 'Not like this, I wasn't.'

Kane looked down at her, still smiling, but his eyes were grave. 'I'm not sure I quite know how to deal with that, my sweet.'

'What . . . what do you mean?'

'I mean, do we carry on or do I retreat gracefully and leave you to your future husband?'

The lazy, casual words conflicted with the unmistakable concern and the affectionate undertones, soothing her initial sense of rejection. Rising up to level with his eyes, her face was glowing now with her radiant, all-giving smile. She felt no need to hide her love for him, her hunger for his body.

'I wouldn't waste any thought on it if I were you. I suggest we just carry on and let the devil take my future husband, unless you're offering yourself as a possible candidate.'

He rose to his feet and pulled her up after him, giving her no answer. She didn't expect one, either. She didn't think she could bear to be any happier than she was at that moment.

She was wrong. She had underestimated her capacity for happiness. It kept expanding hourly, daily, yet she always seemed ready for more.

The time passed in an endless, delirious haze, blurred by her perpetual emotional and physical awareness of Kane, yet with incredible speed the days drifted into weeks. Kane had become a regular member of the Stewart household, adored by her parents, pampered by the servants. And Mrs Stewart's conspiratorial smiles and subtle little attentions already hinted at her eager anticipation of a certain announcement.

Ariel cared nothing for announcements. She just drifted from day to day, reliving the delicious thrill of that first kiss, steeped in a dazed anticipation of the next recurrence. But in spite of her uninhibitedly demonstrative yearnings, Kane never allowed their relationship to go anywhere near that first sensual intimacy which coincided with his first attempt at writing.

Kane was now truly and deeply obsessed with his novel. It was progressing slowly but in a steady, flowing pace, amazing both Ariel and himself by the richness of the plot, the thoughts and ideas hidden behind the light-handed treatment of the genre, the range and depth of the characters. Prospero, the powerful magician, Miranda his daughter, Caliban, Ariel, had all been transformed into modern-day figures, their similarity to the originals more and more blurred and subtle, and the Shakespearian magic was replaced by the more modern concept of space-age, time-travel, computer manipulations and science, which made the book both fascinating, innovative and yet with a certain elusively familiar flavour. It couldn't miss, she told him. It was destined to be a best-seller.

Nevertheless, it was a novel, not a script. And Ariel, trying to maintain the legend of Kane's film career, had by now totally abandoned her own story-writing, and was trying her inexperienced hand at adapting it into a screenplay, using published scripts and professional textbooks as a guide-line. She soon developed a passion for this new form, and was seriously considering a switchover.

So they were now working together in earnest. They practically lived in the improvised beach study, breaking now and again to stretch their muscles with a long swim, skin-diving, or a short spin of water-skiing, and always, as the sun set, they would go jogging along the sandy beaches, venturing, at a more leisurely pace, into the luscious heart of the island. They were only seen at home at dinner, a jealously maintained daily ceremony in the Stewart household.

And they always slept indoors, in their separate

bedrooms, thus soothing any unease in her parents' minds. Kane, Julian and Laura Stewart reassured each other, was honourable to a fault, even if their daughter wasn't. And they were right.

His attitude to her was absent-mindedly affectionate. He was always on his guard against her persisting efforts to draw him any further. He made no secret of his reluctance to get any more involved than he was already. 'It won't do, Ariel,' he patiently explained for the umpteenth time. 'I'd like nothing better than to eat you alive, in fact, I'm aching all over to do so. But the answer is still no, thanks. I can't afford to.'

'Oh, Kane. You're being so unreasonable!'

She had to join him when he burst out laughing. Unreasonable wasn't exactly the word to describe his very commendable aloofness. 'Is that what you would call it?' he chuckled.

'You know what I mean. I love you, I want you, I've never felt like that about any other man and——' She stopped, defeated by his patient, exasperated groan. 'Oh, what's the use, you'll never understand!'

'Oh, I do understand. You would have had to be a very queer sort of a fish if you didn't fall for this mysterious, romantic stranger who descended on your little island like a gift from the sea. And having been introduced to myself only quite recently, I feel quite objective about the man I see in the mirror. Quite an attractive specimen, wouldn't you say?'

She started giggling, her anger as always undermined by his wry, frank humour. 'Oh very . . . that tanned virile body of yours is enough to make any maiden curdle with desire.'

'So you see, my love. For you, it's Miranda and Ferdinand joined together under Prospero's magic power, the ultimate dream-come-true of a love story.' He chuckled as her eyes lit up with hope. 'If you go for Shakespeare's Enchanted Island reality, which I don't, you see.'

Once, only once she made him lose his temper. And the manifestation of his fury was terrifying enough to keep her in check for the rest of the time they had together.

She made the genuinely innocent mistake of rushing into his bedroom one late night, having just come up with a brilliant idea for his novel. She was still fully dressed, but he wasn't. And when her eyes fell on his naked body, lying across the bed without even the thin protection of a sheet, the words stuck in her throat. Carefully she closed the door behind her, turned the key, and approached the bed, her arms, as if independent of her mind, stretched to meet his body.

He was up on his feet in an instant, towering above her, his face cold with fury. His fingers, like a vice, grabbed her by the scruff of her neck and without a word he propelled her to the door. Once there, he unlocked it with his free hand, and practically threw her out, as if she were an undisciplined puppy. 'Wait for me in the shed,' he hissed, glowering down at her, too angry to care if anyone saw him standing naked at the doorway. 'I'll be there as soon as I get dressed. Now go!'

She had never seen him angry before. His was that scathingly cold fury which could paralyse not with any threat of violence, but with the total shutting off of his true, warm self. He was an icy, contemptuous stranger.

'I'll say it once, and no more, Ariel. Don't you ever, ever try that one on me again. I'll make it clear once and for all, you selfish little fool: I am an amnesiac. I know nothing about myself, my past. I could be a criminal, a murderer, a pimp, a . . . Oh, the hell with it, you fill up the blanks. My imagination doesn't stretch far enough. If you're still too thick to follow my meaning, then let me put it this way: when, or if, I ever regain my memory, you might discover that you're chained to a jail-bird, a ruthless mercenary, a psychotic killer . . .'

'You aren't!' she wishpered. 'I know you aren't. And so do you!'

'All right, assuming that you're right . . . how do you feel about being an accessory to a bigamous marriage?'

She looked at him blankly. 'You still don't understand, do you? Damn it, Ariel! I might be already married for all you or I know!'

Ridiculous as it might seem, the thought had never occurred to her.

His face softened, seeing the stricken look on her face. 'So you see, darling, whichever way you look at it, we're stuck. The only solution is to wait and hope that I regain my memory, and then start from scratch. Meanwhile, have mercy on me and stop driving me crazy with provocation. There's a limit to my sense of chivalry. I know your father thinks I'm a true British gentleman at heart, but St Patrick isn't exactly the place to keep reminding me of the fact. And one day . . . one day my self-control will go pop, and I'll have you, flesh, bone and delicious skin. But don't live in hope, Ariel, because so help me,' his voice was lowered now to a hard, dull whisper, 'the day I make love to you, I'll get the hell out of here.'

She looked at him, her eyes wide open, absorbing his threat. 'You can't! You've nowhere to go . . .'

'That's my problem. I mean it, Ariel! If this ever happens, you and this island will never see me again!'

'Never?'

'Well . . .' He couldn't resist the wide-open, distressed gaze. 'Not until I regain my memory and judge myself worthy of your fairy-tale idea of eternal love.'

She didn't give up. Not yet. 'You love me, though. Don't you, Kane? I know you love me, so don't deny it.'

He sighed, turning away from her, and started walking back towards the dark main house. 'If you can trust the feelings of a man who has no past, no future, just a present which consists of one half-finished manuscript of fantasy rubbish, an enchanted island and the feminine version of Shakespeare's Ariel, then yes, I do. I love you. Now, go to bed.'

Her brother's fraternal kiss was more passionate than the one he gave her before he pushed her into her bedroom with a slight slap on the bottom.

For a while she tried to keep herself aloof and haughty, covering every inch of her body, and affecting exaggerated meekness. 'Oh, dear, I do beg your pardon,' she would apologise sarcastically if she as much as crossed her legs in his presence. 'I hope you don't think I'm being provocative.' To which Kane would respond with solemn reassurance: 'Not at all, please feel free to cross your legs whenever you wish.' She was defeated by his unruffled, humorous composure and soon her infectious laughter could be heard again, silvery, bubbling and spontaneously happy.

She learnt to bury her yearnings under a growing absorption in their work, to hide her throbbing need under a light-hearted banter and a perpetual match of wits at which she was becoming very adept under Kane's guidance. So she wasn't to blame for the events which finally shattered the happiest months of her life. As Kane himself was first to admit, it was the gods or perhaps the spirit of Prospero which brought about the eruption of their own personal Tempest.

But whoever's responsibility it was, she lost him. Kane, her fairy-tale love, the man without a past, was gone. And Chris Donahue, the lost computer tycoon assumed dead, re-emerged in the land of the living, to resume where he had left off six months previously, his memory wiped clean of St Patrick and any of the people he had met there. The only tangible souvenirs he carried with him were a haunting memory of a ghost-like laughter and a few hundred pages of an unfinished, untitled fictitious fantasy.

Well, Ariel reminded herself wryly, it was finished now and had a title too: *The Island of the Lost.*

CHAPTER THREE

And now what?

The spacious, impersonal elegance of Chris Donahue's lounge was a cold reminder of the insurmountable gap which existed between the lost man she had known and loved in the enchanted world of her tropical island and the arrogant, celebrated millionaire-turned-writer.

All right, so she had achieved what she set out to do, but now she was totally at a loss as to what she should do next. Somehow she had never thought beyond the point of breaking into Chris Donahue's jealously guarded privacy. This had been the one goal which had kept her going ever since she had found out that he was none other than Kane.

She had never given Kane up. Months after his abrupt departure from St Patrick she kept clinging to her unshaken faith in his love for her, refusing to believe that he had really left her. Deaf to her anxious family's pleading, she buried herself in St Patrick, saw none of her friends, hardly noticed her own family. She even lost interest in her writing. She just went on, barely alive, doggedly working on the script adaptation of his novel, the only tangible heritage he had left behind, and waited, certain that he would come back for her.

It was Michael, home once again on his Christmas holiday and deeply concerned by his sister's emotional condition, who had finally told her about Chris Donahue. He was in London when the English press exploded with headlines and photographs of the missing millionaire's miraculous return to the land of the living. It didn't take him long to identify him as the man they had known as Kane.

'Kane is dead,' he said, almost cruelly, determined to wrench his sister out of her paralysing, hopeless dreams. 'But only to you, just as you are to him. He's found his past, Ariel,' he explained, his voice softening. 'But he's lost you. He's either forgotten or is trying to forget everything that happened to him since he was washed ashore on this island. The press reported that he refused to give any information about the six months he'd been away, but my guess is that he's had another attack of amnesia which left nothing but a black hole of his days in St Patrick.'

Ariel's dead, glazed look frightened him. 'Who is he, Michael?' she asked, her voice hard and flat. 'What's his name? His real name?'

Michael told her all he knew, sparing her nothing. 'So you see, love. It's a lost cause. He doesn't need you now. He's wealthy, successful, a celebrity. He'd be suspicious of anyone who claimed to have known him during his black-out. And even if you did convince him that you were important to him once, I'm sure there's no place for you in his life now. So just accept the facts and try and forget you've ever met him!'

But Ariel didn't. When Michael was ready to go back to England, she left St Patrick with him, determined to fight her way back into Kane's memory no matter what price she would have to pay for it.

She had no trouble whatsoever gathering information about him. As Michael had warned her, he had been quite a celebrity before he disappeared and had become almost a legend since then. She had learnt that he came from an old aristocratic but impoverished family. His parents died in his infancy and he had been brought up by two uncles who had managed to squander the rest of the family's dwindling assets. But with his genius for computers and his incredible business flair, Chris Donahue had brought the Donahue name and fortune far beyond its former glory before he reached thirty, dragging the rest of his idle-rich family with him. To her bitter chagrin, she found out that he had never been married. There were some rumours about an early engagement to some distant relative, a certain Cynthia Donahue, but apparently the engagement had been broken years before his 'mysterious trip', as the press tended to refer to his disappearance.

Applying for a job in Donahue Enterprises seemed to be the best way to get near him. But after a few tedious weeks of temping as a minor typist in the London headquarters, she discovered that Chris Donahue never showed his face in the office. He had lost interest in the business, she was told by a gossip-loving secretary, leaving it in the fumbling hands of his cousin Neville.

She gathered from the numerous articles that Chris Donahue had once been something of a wild jet-setter so she then swallowed her pride and used all her family and social connections, her agent Paul Andrews among them, determined to be introduced to him socially. But here too she seemed to have been barking up the wrong tree. Chris Donahue had apparently dropped out of the social whirl. According to the press, he spent most of his time on his yacht, rarely setting foot in England.

In short, Chris Donahue, for all his fame, was just as inaccessible as Kane.

She had to admit defeat, finally. But by then, she had become more and more involved in her script-writing career, helped along by the gruffly affectionate Paul Andrews, her agent. She was too talented, too vivacious to stay hidden away in her cocoon. There was the challenging thrill of her success as well as all the excitement that London had to offer. And she couldn't help noticing that men found her very attractive even if she herself never felt the slightest temptation to get involved with any of them. So, she patiently waited for the opportunity to meet Kane again, and in the meantime she actually found life rather enjoyable.

And two years later, the opportunity had presented itself. Chris Donahue returned to London, a writer, and by sheer fluke of good fortune, chose Paul Andrews's agency to represent him.

She had been so confident, so naively optimistic when she made her first onslaught on Chris Donahue's blocked memory. And she winced now, remembering the sharp pain and the humiliation which she had felt when she first encountered the writer's blank, impersonal blue gaze. Then, like today, it had dismissed her without a shadow of recollection.

It had happened a few weeks earlier. Paul Andrews and Chris Donahue were having lunch with a certain film producer and the agent had suggested that she

dropped in, as if by chance, so he could introduce
them. It was in the Mayfair, a popular London show-
biz restaurant.

Unlike today, she had done her utmost to look as
much as possible like the beach urchin of her St
Patrick days. She remembered how awkward and silly
she felt in her baggy, slovenly outfit amidst the
restaurant's sophisticated crowd.

Her heart thumping against her ribs, she had
approached their table and waited for Paul Andrews to
introduce her.

Seeing the brilliant blue eyes darken, their cool
indifference ruffled by a momentary bewilderment,
she had thought that her name did penetrate the
writer's dead memory, and foolishly naive, she smiled
at him as she used to in the past, trustingly exposing
her overflowing heart. But there was no answering
smile. His face remained cold and stern until finally her
own smile faltered and faded away in embarrassed
defeat. Stammering her excuses to Paul's invitation to
join them she escaped from the restaurant, barely
checking her tears till she was outside.

It was such a humiliating failure. She had only
managed to arouse Chris Donahue's suspicions and
contempt. Like Paul and the film producer who had
been watching her clumsy attempts to charm him,
Chris thought she was just another star-struck girl,
trying her chance with him.

Yet she still refused to give him up. Obstinately, she
still nourished the hope that even though he had failed
to recognise her face, he was bound to succumb if only
they were allowed to spend some time together,
talking, working, joking with each other as they had
done in the past. And so, when she heard about the
script adaptation of *The Island of the Lost*, she dived in
head first to grab at the last straw of hope.

'Miss Stewart!' Daria's young, high-pitched voice
came from behind her, filtering through the maze of
painful thought. 'Are you all right?'

Ariel looked up, her cheeks covered in a deep blush.

The last thing she needed was to be caught daydreaming, huddled in the writer's favourite lounger. Fortunately, it was the friendly, trusting Daria who had surprised her and not Chris Donahue himself.

'Has Chris been beastly to you?' Daria looked anxiously at the older girl, misinterpreting her unease. 'I'm sorry. He can be such a bully sometimes!'

'Oh, no, no, it's nothing to do with Ka . . . with Mr Donahue,' Ariel stammered, struggling to her feet. 'I wasn't sure whether I was supposed to wait for him. He left rather abruptly, you see.'

Daria's frown cleared at once. 'Oh, that's all right then. You looked so unhappy sitting there, I thought you didn't realise that you've got the job. I've just caught Chris before he zoomed off, and he said you're in. Of course, you know why, don't you?' She gushed on in her disarming, child-like manner, so reminiscent of Ariel's younger self. 'It's your laugh. It's obvious!'

Ariel eyed the girl thoughtfully, marvelling at the girl's instinctive accuracy. 'I hope not,' she laughed, matching the young girl's frivolous tone. 'He must have had better reasons. If it were only my laughter, he could just as well have employed you.'

'Oh, you know what I mean. I'm sure you're a super secretary and all that,' Daria reassured her gravely. 'But I bet it was that laughter of yours. And your name, of course. *The Tempest* happens to be his favourite play.' She suddenly gave the older girl a curious look. 'It's an unusual name for a girl, isn't it? I mean, wasn't Ariel supposed to be a boy?'

Ariel began to edge towards the entrance hall, growing more and more uncomfortable by the girl's observations. ''As a matter of fact it was neither a boy nor a girl,' she mumbled, affecting indifference. 'It was a spirit. And I'd better be going now. We'll have time to chat more tomorrow.'

'Oh no, we won't.' Daria's eyes clouded. 'Once you start working, I won't have any excuse to come here. He doesn't like the family very much and . . . I'm sort of family, you see,' she ended, despondently.

Ariel chuckled. 'Well, he certainly seems to like you.'

'Only because I remind him of someone. You see, he——' Daria stopped and turned a grave look on Ariel. For a moment it seemed as if she was going to blurt out the secret of Chris's loss of memory, but the sound of a car parking outside saved her just in time. 'That would be Marjorie,' she informed her new friend, trapped in her own volatile tendency of hopping from subject to subject. 'You mustn't mind if she isn't too friendly at first. Chris had some . . . well, some trouble with his last secretary and Marjorie tends to be a little suspicious of every woman who comes here. But she's a darling really and I'm sure she'll like you once she gets used to you.' Then she frowned, listening to the quick, staccato sound of high heels hurrying along the paved area outside the front door. 'That doesn't sound like her. I wonder . . .' She stopped and groaned as the door opened without a warning knock. 'Oh bother, it's Cynthia!'

A tawny-maned vision drifted in, shrugging her slender shoulders out of a gold lynx fur coat with the nonchalant grace of a seasoned model. She was one of the most beautiful women Ariel had ever seen but the stunningly lovely face she turned on Ariel was haughty and pained as if she resented her expensive outfit, her sophisticated hair-cut and her young, lovely face.

'Oh hell, Cynthia.' Daria's voice took on a peeved, whiny tone. 'What are you doing here?'

The woman's lovely, immaculately made-up green eyes moved to the young girl. 'Please don't use that tone of voice on me, my girl.' Her voice, like everything else about her, was languid and perfectly modulated. 'You tend to be quite insufferable after five minutes in your uncle's company. Where is he?'

'Out,' Daria answered shortly. 'And this is Ariel Stewart, by the way.' She turned to Ariel with obvious reluctance. 'This is Cynthia Donahue.'

'Cynthia Gordon,' the woman drawled. 'I prefer to hold on to my ex-husband's name. There are far too many Donahue females floating around.' In a flash, Ariel realised this was the 'distant cousin' Chris Donahue was rumoured to have been engaged to in his youth.

The cousins went on talking, ignoring her existence. 'What a nuisance,' Cynthia was saying. 'He said he'd be in this afternoon. I came to talk to him about the weekend party. Did you manage to talk him into it?' Daria shook her head sullenly. 'Why the hell not? After all, it's your birthday party, not mine.'

'I don't want it, nor does Chris and besides you can discuss it with Ariel. She's Chris's new secretary.'

'Oh, are you?' Cynthia responded with a mechanical but nevertheless dazzling smile. 'Well, I hope you'll be an improvement on the last one. Work was the last thing *she* was interested in. Where do you live?'

'London,' Ariel said shortly. She had never been addressed in such a rude, supercilious manner.

The woman looked relieved. 'Well, you won't be living here then.'

Daria burst in, defiantly. 'She will. She's moving in tomorrow. She's going to work with Chris on the adaptation of his novel.'

'Oh really?' The woman gave her a hard look. 'Well, that shouldn't stop you from taking care of my cousin's social engagements. I'll expect you to help with the arrangements for Daria's eighteenth birthday. I'd rather not bother Chris with such matters.' She suddenly seemed a little nervous, in spite of her aloof superiority, and Ariel realised that the woman was quite intimidated by her formidable cousin.

'I'd be delighted,' Ariel said drily, feeling oddly sorry for the beauty. 'Perhaps we can talk about it tomorrow.'

Cynthia hadn't done yet. 'I hope you'll enjoy your job,' she said, rewarding the younger girl with the sweetest smile. 'Chris is a fascinationg man, don't you think?' It was a warning, not a question.

'I've only just met him,' Ariel responded with a polite smile, and walked towards the front door. 'But I know I'll enjoy working on the book. Now, if you'll excuse me . . .'

Cynthia's hard, calculating expression chased her all the way to her car. It seemed that Chris Donahue wasn't the only one to distrust any strange woman who crossed his path. Daria apart, this nasty suspicious streak seemed to be a family trait. She wondered, despondently, whether having returned from his 'trip', Chris had second thoughts about his broken engagement. Few men could resist Cynthia's languid, confident beauty.

Michael, her brother, was already home, showered and refreshed and positively starving, when she finally arrived. 'You're late,' he greeted her accusingly as she walked in. 'I was about to start dinner without you. What kept you?'

Ariel threw her large shoulder-bag and various files on the hall table. 'I had to see someone about a job. And I'm not hungry. You go ahead. I'll grab something later on.'

'Oh no, you don't,' he corrected her. He was six years older and already well established in his medical career, though his attractive freckled face under the shock of bright red hair gave him a deceptively boyish look. 'My cordon bleu chicken deserves some respect. I've been slaving over it for the last half-hour.'

His sister gave in. 'All right, you bully. I'll be down in a minute.'

'Hey,' he called after her, watching her dragging her limbs up the stairs. 'Is anything wrong? You look funny.'

Ariel turned back and stared down at his concerned face. 'Not wrong exactly, but . . .' she hesitated, 'I'll tell you over dinner.'

He let her go at that, slightly uneasy. They were deeply attached and very sensitive to each other's moods, and something about her beaten, despondent air reminded him of those dreadful days on the island after Kane's departure.

She was holding a thick manuscript in publisher's proof form in her hand when she joined him in the small breakfast-room where they usually had their meals.

'What's that?' Michael asked, piling an enormous serving on her plate.

'An unpublished novel,' she said casually. '*The Island of the Lost.*'

'Sounds almost like home, doesn't it?' he chuckled softly. Home was always St Patrick. Neither regarded the gloomy Victorian Dulwich house which they had inherited from their maternal grandparents as a real substitute.

'Ever heard of it?' she asked in the same guarded tone.

'Don't think so.' Her brother's pleasant face remained calm, showing nothing but natural interest in her career. 'Who is it by?'

Ever since she had left Chris Donahue's house she had been deliberating whether to let Michael in on her secret. Here was her chance but something held her back. Until now, she had shared with him all her plans concerning Kane, involved him in her soaring hopes and crying on his shoulder after each heart-wrenching failure. It seemed unfair to involve him with yet another wild goose-chase. Besides, feeling despondent and defeated as she had done since her interview, she didn't think she could stand Michael's justified scoffing at the stupidity of her latest charade. 'Oh, you wouldn't know him.' she said at last. 'It's his first novel.'

'Where you commissioned to do the adaptation?'

Ariel's guarded expression relaxed. 'Not really. I'm only a ghost. Not even that ... call it a dogsbody with the rather fancy title of secretary. I like the book,' she went on, volunteering the information before he could question her odd choice of a job. 'And I need the experience. Anyway, the job isn't mine yet. I'm on trial.'

She stood up and started collecting the dirty dishes, avoiding his narrowed, thoughtful eyes.

Michael's uneasy feeling deepened as he watched her later on, settled on the sofa by the blazing fireplace, engrossed in her reading. She was going through the thick, unbound manuscript, discarding the pages one by one with astonishing speed, stopping only now and again to make a note in a small pad.

'Aren't you going a bit fast?' he asked her finally, noting the high pile of discarded pages on the floor. 'I can't believe you could take all that in one short hour.'

Ariel looked up, taking a few seconds to focus her attention on her brother's remark. 'Oh, I only need to read the last few chapters,' she said lightly. 'I'm only checking through the first part for any changes from the original version.' And smiling at him vaguely, she returned to the manuscript.

'You did say it was an unpublished novel, didn't you?' Michael asked casually.

'Yes, it's due out in six weeks, I think.'

She was utterly unprepared for his next remark. 'You have known the writer for quite a while, I gather?'

Ariel's head jerked up in astonishment. 'What . . . what makes you say that?'

Michael's eyes were studying her with something very near suspicion. 'How else can you explain the fact that you're so well acquainted with the original version of his novel.'

For a moment she felt tempted to spill it all out, but then decided to stick by her initial decision. She had to go through with this alone, this time.

'Do you want to tell me about it?' he prompted gently.

She shook her head. 'Not yet, Michael. Not before I know where I stand.'

Paul Andrews phoned her later on that evening. He had obviously been speaking to Chris Donahue and could supply her with all the practical details which the writer forgot or refused to discuss with her. She didn't need his wry confirmation that her chances of keeping the job were very flimsy indeed.

'I'm not cancelling any of your contracts yet, Ariel,' he said drily. 'Donahue's determined to leave London in about ten days' time and by that time we'll know whether you're in or out. You'll have to make yourself bloody indispensable if you want to go on with the adaptation.'

'I know,' she sighed, too tired to reassure him. 'I don't think he relishes the prospect of spending several weeks alone with me aboard his yacht. In fact, one hour was too much for him.'

There was a slight pause at the other end. 'Did he give you a hard time?' the elderly agent asked, gently. 'You mustn't mind him, my dear. He's a great chap, you know, far nicer than he makes out. He just had to build a very hard shell around himself ever since— Oh, never mind.' He stopped, abruptly.

'I know about his loss of memory, Paul,' she said quietly, guessing his reason for clamming up. 'He told me.'

'He did?' The agent sounded surprised, even impressed. 'Well, at least he trusts you.'

Ariel laughed bitterly. 'Oh no, he doesn't. He thinks I'm after him, or his money or God knows what.' Her misery now erupted in full force. 'He's the most insufferable, arrogant, suspicious bully I've ever come a——'

'He's got his reasons, darling.' The dry voice tried to cool down her furious outburst. 'He's been besieged by people, women mostly, pretending to have known him during those lost months, attempting to blackmail him with the most outrageous stories. If he were to believe them, he must have had a dozen wives at least, let alone fathered scores of children . . .'

'Good heavens.' Ariel was taken aback. 'I never thought of that. I thought no one was supposed to know about it . . .'

'It wasn't publicised in the press, fortunately. But Chris made the mistake of sending detectives and investigators to every island in the Indian Ocean, trying to find out what had happened to him during the months that followed his plane crash, which was the last thing he remembered before he blacked out. Naturally, a good number of people couldn't resist the chance of cashing in. He sussed them out, of course, but you can't blame him for being suspicious and cautious now. Especially with someone like you.'

'What do you mean, someone like me?' Ariel interrupted, bristling.

'Well, you're young, extremely attractive and, if you'll forgive an old man for saying so, you haven't been too subtle about the way you went about trying to draw his attention. And above all, my dear, he knows you come from the Seychelles Islands. So what can you expect?'

Ariel groaned, miserably. 'No more than I got, I guess. I'm beginning to understand now why I got the fish-eye from his family as well.'

'Not little Daria, surely?'

'Oh, not her. But one of his cousins——' She refrained from mentioning Cynthia by name, afraid of what she might hear. 'I was practically warned to keep my hands off him.'

Paul Andrews stopped her. 'Don't worry about his family. The less they like you the better. He makes no secret of his dislike and distrust of them. And no wonder, they behaved shamefully during the time he'd been missing and when he came back.'

'Come now, Paul. Surely, they were overjoyed to have him back?'

'You couldn't be more wrong. They were quite upset when they realised that they'd have to let go of the money they thought was theirs. Even Neville, whom he had always treated as a brother, was far too in love with his position as the new head of the Donahue Empire to receive the news of Chris's return from the dead with great pleasure. It's not a real family, Ariel. Just cousins and distant relatives who've been sponging off Chris for years.'

'I . . . I didn't know, Paul. How awful.' It had never occurred to her that Kane's return to his old life had brought its own problems and unhappiness. In a way, she suddenly realised, it must have been almost as shattering and bewildering as his waking up in a strange island without a past or identity. She had been so immersed in her own misery and sense of loss that she had never given a thought to his ordeal.

She sighed. 'I wish I'd never talked you into getting me that interview!'

'Well, it's too late now, Ariel. You'll have to go along with it and for my sake, don't make him regret his decision. After all, it was me who recommended you. I practically coerced him into it. Besides,' he ended, once again the seasoned wily agent, 'you may still end up doing the adaptation with him, which is the point of the whole exercise as far as I'm concerned. Have you read the book yet?'

'Don't worry. I'll finish it even if it takes me the whole night.'

'Good girl, just as long as you get some sleep. You'll need all your wits about you tomorrow, my dear. If you think Chris Donahue was tough today, you just wait and see what's in store for you once you start working with him.'

CHAPTER FOUR

IT WAS Marjorie, a dumpy little Irish middle-aged woman, who let her in next morning. She had obviously been briefed by their mutual employer, because before Ariel could think of a proper way to introduce herself, the loyal housekeeper made it quite clear that even though Ariel was a very welcome addition to the 'staff', she was expected to keep out of Mr Christopher's way.

'I'm sure you'll find here all you need, my dear,' she said in her soft Irish brogue as she showed Ariel to a large spare bedroom which was equipped with a small TV set, books, even a music-centre; in fact, Ariel remarked wryly to herself, it made quite sure that she'd have no excuse to look for entertainment elsewhere in the house.

'Mr Christopher prefers to eat in his part of the house,' the housekeeper went on awkwardly, attempting to soften her employer's blunt instructions. 'So I hope you won't mind having your meals alone. And you can always join me in the kitchen if you feel like company. It would be so nice to chat with someone who is not interested only in gossip . . . like young Daria, I mean,' she ended hurriedly, in case Ariel took offence at her unsubtle hint.

'She is a bit of a chatterbox, isn't she?' Ariel agreed with her reassuringly. 'And it's a lovely room. I'm quite overwhelmed, in fact,' she went on, inspecting the impersonal elegance of her temporary new lodgings with its adjoining luxurious bathroom, 'I'm sure I'll be perfectly comfortable here. After all, it's only for a few days, isn't it?'

The elderly woman seemed to relax a little now that the unpleasant part of her task was accomplished. And with touching pride she set out to show Ariel the rest of her kingdom, ending in Ariel's own domain: the study.

'Mr Christopher says you can use this room whenever you like. His own rooms are at the other side of the villa so you needn't worry about disturbing him.'

It was a lovely, airy room, smaller and cosier than the huge lounge with which it shared the enchanting trellised patio and the spectacular view over the gentle green slopes and the sparkling pond of Hampstead Heath.

The only concession towards functionalism was the buff-coloured, streamlined office desk and the matching filing-units which blended well with the room. Ariel's admiring eyes went straight to the Donahue Personal Computer which was positioned on a custom-made stand. It was a Rolls-Royce compared to her own battered portable computer. She chuckled to herself, thinking of her secret collaborator, who had so loyally been covering up for her atrocious typing, hopeless spelling and disorganised writing habits throughout her three-year career.

'Mr Christopher will be here shortly. He asked me to tell you that you might start by getting to grips with his computer and to let me know if there's anything else you might need.' Marjorie reported her final instruction word for word, obviously at sea when it came to her employer's professional activities.

'Nothing at all,' Ariel reassured her. 'It's perfect.'

Briskly, she walked to the desk, sat down in the comfortable, high-backed swivel chair and turned on the computer. Then, with a dismissing but friendly smile, she pretended to become absorbed by the unfamiliar system.

It had been a deliberate manoeuvre to reassure Marjorie of her utter lack of interest in anything but the work she had been hired to do. And stealthily watching Marjorie from the corner of her eyes, she concluded from the woman's relaxed, approving expression that she had achieved her goal. Not that Chris Donahue would in any way be influenced by the housekeeper's favourable impression, but it would make her stay in the house far more pleasant.

It was long past eleven when her new employer strode into the room, rewarding her polite morning greeting with a disgruntled mumble which could be taken as a certain acquiescence to basic manners. Chris Donahue's temper wasn't at its best in the morning. That much he still had in common with Kane.

He was dressed with the same characteristic off-hand elegance and had taken the trouble to shave but his heavy eyes and the sour set of his mouth indicated a late night and probably quite a few drinks. He winced at the sight of that lovely, animated face, smiling with obvious anticipation of the start of their first working day.

'Forget it,' he said heavily. 'I hadn't planned on plunging in today. You just get on with reading the manuscript. I don't suppose you've had time to really look at it.'

She broke in cheerfully, 'Oh, but I have, Mr Donahue, I finished it la——'

His exasperated grimace stopped the ready chatter. 'Cut the Mr Donahue bit. My name is Chris. I thought we'd already been over that one yesterday.' The cold voice was clearly warning her to stick to the rules. She was temporarily employed to do a certain job, and he had only agreed to tolerate her for a trial period. He had neither the time nor the inclination for games or for her friendly charm.

'Certainly. I'm sorry . . .' she responded placidly, determined not to let his bad temper ruffle her. 'I

finished reading it last night, Chris. Not in depth, of
course, but enough to get the general idea.'

He was taken aback. 'Well, that's quite a feat,
considering the fact that it sprawls over five hundred
pages.'

Ariel accepted his grudging compliment with a
flicker of an eyelid. In fact she had had to read less
than two hundred pages, those that had been written
over the last three years. She had only scanned
through the earlier part which she knew almost by
heart, or so she thought. Very soon she had cause to
regret her frivolous boast. He had made quite a few
significant changes in his old St Patrick version and
she could have easily betrayed herself by referring to
characters and events which no longer existed.
Fortunately, after the first narrow escape, she was
careful not to volunteer anything before hearing him
refer to it first.

'We might as well begin, then,' Chris suggested,
with a marked lack of enthusiam.

Ariel gave her new boss a cool, polite smile, and said
nothing.

There was a long pause. He was evidently at a loss
as to where or how to begin, and Ariel was determined
not to make it easier for him. He finally broke the
silence with a rueful smile. 'You'd better make the
first move, Ariel. I've never had to collaborate on a
script before.'

'Well,' she gracefully accepted his disarming
admission of defeat, 'you may want to have a look at
my draft for what seemed to me like a possible
opening.' She handed over the scant computer print-
out. 'I worked on it this morning,' she explained, with
studied indifference.

If he was impressed by her extraordinary productivity,
he gave no sign of it. 'I see you had no trouble getting to
grips with my computer,' was all the praise he was
prepared to offer. 'Which one do you use yourself?'

She mentioned the make and he mumbled his approval. 'Plodding but dependable. Excuse me.' Not bothering to sit down, he began to scan over the few pages.

She held her breath, closely watching his face from under her lowered eyelashes for any sign of recognition, half dreading, half hoping that he would catch her lie. It was the first scene of the original adaptation which she and Kane had worked on in St Patrick. All she had done this morning was to copy it into Chris's computer, word for word. If Kane was lurking somewhere in his subconscious memory, he would have recognised it instantly.

But Chris's eyes, when he finally raised them from the pages, looked untroubled by any shadow of half-buried memory. 'Yes, I like that,' he said calmly. 'It makes an intriguing opening without giving out too much. And you managed to hint at the hidden powers of Gavillan while maintaining a first impression of an ordinary man. We'll keep it. My only reservation is your treatment of the girl, Alexis. I suggest we stick to my version of it.'

'But I did!' she protested, taken aback.

'Well, it certainly doesn't show. Your Alexis is very charming, I admit, but I find her far too humane and dizzy for a female humanoid.'

'A female humanoid?' She frowned, puzzled.

He gave her a long, narrow look. 'Are you sure you've read the novel? I mean, *my* novel? Or are you writing your own?'

Frantically, she scanned through the first few chapters in her mind. 'Sorry, Chris,' she said finally. 'But I really don't know what you're talking about.'

'I'm talking about Alexis,' he intoned, patiently, as if she were a backward child. 'Gavillan's creation . . . A human robot . . . a female clone!' He finally exploded. 'The humanoid Alexis, damn it!'

Ariel's puzzled frown cleared at last. Alexis of the original version had been based on Shakespeare's mischievous sprite, Ariel, with very dominant characteristics of herself. There certainly had never been any hint of a man-made humanoid clone. In her hasty, over-confident reading of the book, she had somehow overlooked the significant change he had made in his final version.

'I'm sorry,' she said coldly. 'I told you I went through the book very quickly. It just never occurred to me that she was a humanoid.' Inside she was seething with rage at what he had done to his subconscious memory of her.

'I wonder how the fact could have escaped you. I thought it was pretty obvious.'

The only way out was to attack back. 'Well, you couldn't have been very convincing about her being a humanoid. Alexis seemed extremely human to me.'

He didn't speak for a long moment. 'Did she?' he said finally, almost menacing.

'Yes. And at the risk of speaking out of turn, I think it was a mistake to make her a man-made machine, in the first place. There's precious little human warmth and emotion in your book as it is.'

She had gone too far. Paul Andrews had warned her to keep her opinions to herself, to curb her own creative imagination. Her job was purely technical. The genius was to be Chris Donahue's alone. Resigned, she waited for his explosive reaction and her prompt dismissal.

But his reaction was as unpredictable as everything else about him. 'All right,' he said, quite mildly. 'We'll keep it for now. I'll go over it more carefully later.'

Silently, she gloated with well-earned smugness. This was their first wrestling match today, and this time at least she came out the winner.

Chris threw the printed pages on to the low coffee-table, and settled comfortably on the Eames leather lounger, his long legs resting on the matching stool. These, then, were to be their working positions. He, lazily sprawling by the glazed wall, enjoying the green landscape of the Heath, while she, sitting upright behind the desk, was to face the blinking monitor. No eye contact as far as possible, she remarked wryly to herself.

'Right,' he went on, picking up his own manuscript. 'Let's get on with it, shall we? I think I know where to go from here.'

Ariel sat up, her hands on the keyboard of the

glamorous computer, ready to go. A picture of the alert, impersonal secretary.

'Interior or exterior?' she asked wickedly.

'I beg your pardon?'

'We're supposed to head every scene with the basic details, you know ... Day or Night, Exterior or Interior, etc. Which scene are we going into next then?'

His cool glance told her that he was on to her malicious intention to expose his ignorance in the medium. 'I'll leave you to supply all the technical buzz-words,' he said calmly. 'I'll catch on in a few days, I dare say. For the moment, let's just concentrate on a general break-down and a rough outline of the whole script. Somehow, in my ignorance, I assumed that this should be our first concern.'

A furious blush covered Ariel's cheeks as she squirmed with embarrassment. He was right, of course. That was invariably the very first stage, and she could have told him so in her sleep had she not been so stupidly eager to astound him with her cleverness. Her moment of smug superiority was very brief indeed.

'But you are the expert, of course, so I'm very happy to be guided by you,' he went on, taunting her, malicious dig for malicious dig.

She shook her head dumbly, feeling utterly stupid. She should have known better, she scolded herself furiously. Chris Donahue would always have the upper hand, just as Kane had.

'Can we begin then?' he suggested.

It was a slow, awkward start. Seated so far apart, as distant from each other as the room would allow, she was forced to leave her desk every few minutes, cross over to the Eames lounger where Chris was sprawling, to check his break-down charts and compare them with her own, since verbal references were far too vague. Moreover, this obliged her to bend down over him, and her shoulders and back muscles were beginning to ache with tension, as she had to keep constant guard against making any accidental contact with his body. Chris, utterly relaxed and unconcerned with her particular discomfort, was nevertheless obliged to read out whole sections from his manuscript so that she could follow his suggestions for a possible link or break between episodes. He soon got thoroughly fed up, as his listless, exasperated voice indicated.

Finally, on her tenth journey across the room, Ariel stopped dead in her tracks, and against her better judgement, burst out laughing. This was ridiculous.

Her breathless laughter was joined, unexpectedly, by a low, well-remembered chuckle. 'I quite agree. This is getting us nowhere fast. So, all right, Clever Dick,' he stood up, throwing his manuscript on the floor, 'how do you suggest we do it then?'

At last, they had reached some sort of a truce. Whatever he was before and after his temporary amnesia, he still retained Kane's wry humour and the knack of self-ridicule. And it seemed that both personalities were rendered quite powerless by Ariel's ultimate weapon: her irrepressible laughter.

She drew out a simple, sensible plan and once she got his approval, left him only long enough to get out of the ridiculous sophisticated outfit she had donned that morning in her capacity as an executive secretary, and threw on her favourite baggy cords and a huge, loosely knitted cotton jumper which almost buried her lithe body, all the way down to her slim hips.

Now, they fell to work in earnest, almost effortlessly slipping into their St Patrick collaborating routine. The frosty, hostile atmosphere in the room was beginning to buzz with escalating excitement, warmed by bursts of chuckles and the fast, well-matched banter at which they had always been so good. It was obvious that they still shared that uncanny unique empathy which made each read the other's thoughts and ideas almost before they could be formed into words.

When Marjorie walked in, carrying a large tray of sandwiches and a fresh pot of coffee, she found the study in total shambles. All the furniture had been pushed to the wall, leaving the centre of the room uncluttered. Her employer was lying flat on his stomach, while his new assistant, in shabby cords and a huge jumper, was crawling around organising and reorganising the crumpled notes and pages which covered every inch of the thick ivory carpet. She watched them for a moment, astounded. She hadn't seen Mr Chris looking so relaxed since his return from that hellish journey of his.

'Ah, Marjorie,' Chris greeted the older woman with a wide smile. 'I was just about to holler for more coffee.'

With something of a shock, Ariel surfaced from her total absorption in their work, to realise she had actually forgotten that as far as Chris Donahue was concerned, she was still a total stranger. What's more, that she herself hadn't given one single thought to Kane.

'It's nearly two o'clock, Mr Chris. I insist you stop now and have something to eat,' the elderly housekeeper stated firmly, looking around helplessly for a clear path to the the coffee-table.

'Leave us alone, Marge . . . and you can take the sandwiches with you. I don't want them.'

Ariel gave him a scathing look. She had had her breakfast at eight, and she was starving.

'You may not be hungry, Mr Chris, but the girl hasn't had anything since she arrived here,' the housekeeper scolded him sternly. 'I'll leave the tray here, by the sofa. You'll have to find your own way through this mess to get it.' And with a last despairing glance at the chaotic mess, she left the room.

Winding her way through a hurdle course of crumpled charts and manuscript pages, Ariel attacked the delicious-looking sandwiches, refusing to be intimidated by her boss's workaholic lack of consideration.

A soft, lazy chuckle reached her from across the room, sending a shiver through her body, as if aroused by a physical caress. Cautiously, almost afraid of what she might see in his face, she turned around towards him.

He was sitting up, his back leaning against the desk, studying her with that well-remembered heart-wrenching lazy amusement. Once again, like the day before, her Kane, the man she had known and loved in St Patrick, was peering at her from behind the cool, remote shell which was Chris Donahue.

'And I thought spirits never ate . . .' he said casually, and the food stuck in her throat. 'But then you're no spirit, are you? Quite exasperatingly human, I gather.'

It couldn't be happening, she kept saying to herself again and again. She must be day-dreaming. In a few casual, teasing words, he leaped across all the barriers, all the years which had separated them. Her blood racing madly through her veins, she forced herself to remain where she was, her face clean of all expression, and with wide, unblinking eyes, waited for his next move.

But nothing happened. The man was looking at her with the pleasant smile of a friendly stranger, totally unaware of the extraordinary words he had just uttered. It was as if Kane's ghost had used Chris's body as a medium to communicate with her.

'Well, eat up, woman.' His voice was still warm and lazy as Kane's, but the dry exasperation was that of Chris Donahue. 'And pour me a cup of coffee while you're at it. I want to get on with this.'

As if pierced by a sharp knife, her arrested breath came out in a low audible groan. Disappointment hit her like a physical blow, leaving her faint and profoundly shaken.

'Hey, are you all right?' He sat up, instantly alert by the sick pallor of her cheeks. 'I'm sorry, darling. You'd better stop now and have some rest. We'll continue later.'

She managed to swallow at last, but put the rest of the half-eaten sandwich back on the tray. 'No, let's go on. I'm fine. Really.'

'All right, then.' He didn't insist. 'Bring your sandwiches over here. You can eat and work at the same time, can't you?'

The moment passed. It was so brief she began to

think she had imagined the whole thing. On unsteady feet, she tip-toed back to her old place, beside his long, loose-limbed body, and with superhuman effort, managed to shake clear of her momentary shock and force her mind to concentrate on the task ahead. It was an old remedy, she reminded herself. Kane had taught her to bury her relentless yearnings for him in the frenzy of creative work which transformed him from a lover into a colleague. And at least, in this case, her relationship with Chris was hardly any different. Work was her only safe anchor, and it did bring them as close together as she could ever hope to be.

They worked tirelessly, obsessively throughout the day, and late into the evening. Marjorie's frequent interruptions, insisting they stopped for a hot meal, were waved aside absent-mindedly. It was past nine when Chris finally sat up, stretched his arms and arched his broad back in an old familiar gesture which wrenched Ariel's insides in another stabbing pang of unbearable yearnings, and announced that he could do with a short jog.

'Thank God,' she said coolly. 'I was beginning to think you weren't prone to such human frailties as weariness.'

They were sitting very close together, peering over the final draft of their provisional break-down chart, feeling rather pleased with their achievement. 'What an inconsiderate brute I am, sweetheart.' He turned to her, touching her arm in a natural, friendly gesture of apology. Ariel stiffened involuntarily, jerking her arm away. 'Next time,' he went on, pretending not to notice her almost rude withdrawal. 'Next time, you'd better stop me when you feel I'm driving you too hard. I did give you a fair warning yesterday, didn't I? I tend to ignore other people when I work. No, scrap that, I tend to ignore other people, period.'

'I don't think so.' She spoke softly, more to herself than to him. 'I don't think you're as unfeeling and cold as you make out to be.'

'That's very sweet of you, darling, but I am, and you had better believe it. Now how about that run?'

She noticed that he took it for granted that she was a regular jogger. Once again, without his realising it, his deeply buried memory was playing up, independent of his conscious mind.

With an effortless pull, he helped her up to her feet, still with the same casual camaraderie with which he had touched her arm before. This time, she didn't withdraw her hand. Careful not to show any of her feelings, she followed him out of the study patio doors to the wooden gate at the end of the villa's garden which led them across the narrow public path into the Heath. Nothing could be more different from the sandy beaches of St Patrick than the dark London night and the wet grass under their sneakers. Yet, as if triggered by the same inner mechanism, they broke together into a slow, leisurely jog side by side, just as they used to do years ago, on her island.

It wasn't very cold but the wind was rising quickly, its whining sound heralding a coming storm. But neither she nor Chris let it deter them. She was used to the sudden drenching rains and so was he, if he retained some inner memories of his life on St Patrick.

They jogged past the sleepy pond all the way to Kenwood Park, and back again. It was a short run compared to the miles they were used to but she was out of breath, panting like a thirsty puppy, when they reached the dark villa.

'I'm out of practice,' she panted apologetically, struggling to catch her breath. 'I have hardly moved a muscle since coming to London.'

'How long ago was that?'

'Oh, three years, or thereabouts.'

'From the Seychelles, isn't that right? What was that island again?'

'St Patrick,' she said lightly.

'Oh yes . . .' The thin drizzle had developed into a proper shower now, hitting their flushed bodies with tiny ice droplets just as they reached the wide paved area at the front of the house. Putting a light protective arm around her waist, Chris hurried her up the shallow stairs and into the quiet house. But the minute they were safe inside, his arm dropped abruptly, in what seemed to Ariel a sudden distaste.

Looking straight ahead, so as not to show how stupidly shaken she had been even by such remote, impersonal contact, she couldn't see the shadow of bewildered anguish which clouded his face and the startled way he looked down on his arm, as if it had just been touched by a live electric wire.

She was already striding towards the kitchen quarters where poor Marjorie was still waiting to feed them, when she realised that he was going in the other direction.

'Tell Marjorie I'll have something simple in my room, will you?' he said, over his shoulder. 'I don't feel like a full meal.'

She stopped short, stunned by his abrupt, rude withdrawal when she least expected it. 'She has been keeping that meal warm for you all evening, you know,' she said coldly. 'Don't you think you owe her some consideration?'

'If I do, it's between her and me. I really don't see how my habits are any concern of yours. Unless you are incapable of spending what's left of the evening in your own company.'

Ariel bristled. 'Don't let that bother you. I have spent most of my life on an island with only my brother and my parents for company. So, believe me, I am quite used to being on my own. Good night!'

It took her several minutes before she managed to soothe her hurt pride and indignation. He would have treated a duchess with the same off-hand disregard, she reminded herself. Chris Donahue cared nothing for drawing-room manners. Nor did Kane, for that matter. They both did exactly what they felt like. The difference was that Kane would have certainly felt like staying with her the whole night, loving her, waking up beside her in the morning and letting her drag him out of bed to carry on with their work. While Chris just withdrew into his lonely, cold shell . . . perhaps to flog his impaired memory with relentless questioning, desperate to find the man who sank into the black hole of oblivion.

Marjorie was obviously used to his treatment. 'Don't let it upset you, dear. He needs to be alone when the dark mood gets him. And don't you worry about me. I have precious little to do as it is, what with Mr Chris being away most of the year. I'd rather have his irregular hours and moods than Mrs Grace's finicky habits.'

The storm outside had erupted in full scale when Ariel had at last finished eating and was allowed to retreat into the privacy of her comfortable, impersonal bedroom, too drained, too exhausted to change into her nightgown, or even crawl under the covers. Her ears and mind were whirring with the sounds of the howling wind and the lashing rain outside the huge uncurtained windows. She just sat on the large bed, thinking about Chris, shut away in his own private hell, and wondering whether his senses or his impulses, whatever it was that was not governed by his conscious mind, were stirred like hers by the memory of another night and another storm, far more vicious and sinister than this mild English copy-cat, which had brought about the eruption of their repressed passion.

CHAPTER FIVE

IT was the eerie, heavy silence which had awakened Ariel that night. She lay still in her bed, instantly interpreting the cause of her unease as the suffocating stillness which usually preceded an oncoming storm. Serious gales rarely broke out at this time of year, so like her parents and the locals, all seasoned St Patrick natives, she disregarded the warning bell of her instincts. Just a storm, she decided, and was about to drift back into sleep when the sound of her mother's pitiful groans reached her through the thin wall which separated her parents' bedroom from hers.

When Ariel reached her mother's side, Julian

Stewart was already on the phone, summoning a helicopter to fly him and his wife to Mahe, for an emergency operation. Laura Stewart was in pain, bad pain. There was no need for a doctor to diagnose her fierce nausea and the sharp, unrelenting pangs in her right side as an acute appendicitis attack. Living in the isolation of their island, the Stewarts had to be well informed and always alert to any alarming signs of illness.

In less than twenty minutes, the small hospital chopper landed on the Stewart garden's primitive landing platform and Kane, calm and reassuring, carried Laura in his arms down the steps and settled her as comfortably as her pain would allow, on the stretcher.

'I'll call the moment I have any news,' Julian Stewart promised Ariel. 'Meanwhile, you'd better put up the storm shutters. I think we're in for a good storm.'

The chopper pilot calculated at least an hour before the storm broke out in earnest, time enough for him to deposit his suffering passenger in the Mahe hospital.

They waited only long enough to see the chopper take off before they started preparing for the storm. Right season or not, the drill always took the precaution of preparing for the eventuality of a major gale. Dispensing with the help of the servants who had their own homes to worry about, she and Kane had the house well prepared for whatever lashing the unpredictable weather held in store.

Her father rang an hour later to tell her that they had reached the hospital safely, and her mother was now undergoing the operation. They'd caught it just in time, before it burst.

It was two o'clock before she and Kane retired to their respective bedrooms and Ariel was too exhausted by her midnight exertions and too preoccupied with her mother's condition to digest the fact that for the first time since Kane's arrival, she and he were utterly alone in the large house.

She was awakened after two hours of fitful sleep, all

her instincts alerted by the furious lashing of the rain against the storm shutters and the alarming sound of the whirling wind. In an instant, she suddenly remembered Kane's manuscript and her own script adaptation, carelessly stacked away in the flimsy wooden cabinet of her shed.

She knew better than to leave the shelter of the house during a storm, but the thought of leaving those precious pages to the mercy of the wind and the rain overcame her initial sensible caution.

Throwing her clothes on, she rushed out of her room, pausing outside Kane's room. For a moment she considered waking him up so as not to be forced to make her way down to the beach alone, but suspecting he would try to prevent her from coming along, decided to carry on on her own.

She had to struggle with the narrow kitchen back door against the furiously flowing wind, and was immediately hit by the torrent of ice-cold rain, which hit her face in an avalanche of tiny sharp daggers. The wind was blowing against her, howling like a wounded animal, fighting her every inch of the way as she took the steep steps down to the beach. She should have taken one of the oilskins which were kept in the main hall, but it was too late now. She was already drenched to the bones, shuddering with cold, her body a pathetic barrier against the hammering rain.

Half way down, she stopped, overwhelmed by the terror of the mad world into which she had stumbled. It was not an ordinary storm. She had no doubt now that this was a major gale, perhaps even the tail-end of a cyclone. Paralysed by indecision, she remained fixed to the spot, too far from the shed yet not near enough to retrace her steps and return to the shelter of the house.

Suddenly, a large shadowy figure emerged out of the black whirling hell, making her faint with a momentary terror. Her feet lost their grip on the slippery stone steps and she began to fall forwards, with nothing to arrest the head-on tumble down, down, into the black abyss of whirling air.

Next moment, she was held safe and steady against Kane's dripping oilskin.

'You idiot,' he shouted against the deafening howl of the wind. 'What are you doing out here?'

'The manuscript!' She had to scream to be heard. 'My script . . . down in the shed!'

'I've got them!' he yelled back, thrusting a bulky parcel wrapped in oilskin into her arms. And suddenly, her feet were dangling in the air, as he grabbed her by the waist, and tucked her under his arm as if she were a limp puppet.

It had taken Ariel a good twenty minutes to reach this point, going down. Now, climbing back in the direction of the gale, Kane was outside the kitchen door in less than five minutes, almost swept off his feet by the force of the wind.

Once outside the house, he deposited her back on the ground, making sure her hand was clasped securely around the iron grilles of the small back veranda, while he himself struggled to keep the kitchen door from being wrenched off its hinges. With what seemed like superhuman strength, he held it half open with one arm, and then, ordering her to let go of the grille, pulled her inside, himself following immediately and pushing the door shut against the angry whine of the wind.

The house was rocking and shuddering, promising a very flimsy protection against the raging elements outside. The air was unpleasantly damp and chilly. But at least, the manuscript and her adaptation were safe, if somewhat soggy, on the kitchen table.

'Next time you decide to play Pygmalion to some poor, unsuspecting victim, you'd better make sure he makes a carbon copy of his creative genius,' he said drily, busily peeling off his dripping oilskin. 'You're soaked, you idiot,' he announced, and then added grimly, So am I, come to think of it. Where's the light switch?'

She left him, groping her way in the darkness to reach for the switch. Nothing happened. 'Forget it,' she said, resigned. 'The generator hardly ever functions in such storms. You'll find the kerosene lamp behind you, on the top shelf. It should be full. The matches are next to it.'

Every house in the islands had to be kept in constant readiness for such eventualities. She could hear him fumbling with the primitive lamp and after a few minutes and a flood of hissing curses, the kitchen came alive with the dim, melancholy light of the single pale flame.

'Fireplace . . . I don't remember seeing one anywhere in the house,' he remarked, as if to himself.

'This isn't England, you know. We never need heating in St Patrick.' She spoke shortly, already busy with the old-fashioned Aga stove, which was kept for such times when the generator failed to supply electricity for the up-to-date oven.

The pleasant heat made her even more aware of the discomfort of her sodden clothes. 'There are some blankets in the cupboard in the main hall. You'd better take off your clothes, while I bring them in,' she suggested mildly.

She had no trouble finding her way in the pitch darkness. In a few minutes, she was back in the kitchen, carrying an armload of fluffy mohair covers, and a bottle of her father's best Scotch.

'I thought you'd appreciate that,' she giggled, feeling better now that she was being mistress of the situation. She was used to these gales, after all. Kane wasn't.

He had only removed his wet shirt, and was standing by the Aga stove, rubbing his chilled body vigorously with a tea-towel. The dim light of the lamp hit the smooth skin of his lean, powerful back. She couldn't take her eyes off the fascinating play of his rippling muscles.

He seemed to have eyes in the back of his head. 'Stop gaping, Ariel, and get out of those clothes!' he startled her by saying impatiently.

Shaking herself, she threw him one of the blankets, and began to remove her wet sweat-shirt and her tight jeans which clung unpleasantly to her legs, refusing to come off.

He was suddenly kneeling in front of her, his exasperated hands pushing hers out of the way as he tugged at the soggy jeans, pulling them down and lightly slapping each foot in turn, silently ordering her to lift it while he slipped the trousers off.

Having completed the task, still kneeling in front of her, he straightened up to grab the mohair blanket he had left on the table behind. He was about to wrap it around her when he stopped short. To her deep, shivering embarrassment, she only just remembered that she hadn't bothered with any underwear when she hurriedly threw on her clothes, before rushing out into the storm.

His hand, holding the soft blanket, was arrested a few inches away from her defenceless nakedness. Time seemed to stand still, as both remained motionless. Then, with a feeble, awkward gesture, she put her hand forward to take the blanket from his hand and cover herself up. But instead of passing it to her, and turning away in angry disgust as she expected him to do, he let drop the soft material, and caught her hand in his, forbidding it to protect herself from his gaze.

'Oh God, Kane,' she whispered, feeling guilty and ashamed even though she was hardly to blame for her predicament. 'I'm sorry . . . I didn't mean to——'

'Hush, kitten,' was all he said. And his eyes rose to meet hers, hungry, naked yet with a glint of wry humour. 'We're in the hands of the gods now, I guess. No point trying to fight them, is there?'

She still didn't dare to believe she read his meaning correctly. He hadn't even touched her. 'You're not angry, then?' she asked.

He ignored her question. 'Go on, Ariel. Just cover yourself up in that blasted blanket and let's go upstairs. I don't think we'll need that Aga stove to keep away the cold any more.'

Confused by his cool, matter-of-fact tone, she still wasn't sure she had actually managed to crack the hard shield of his self-control. 'Come on, Ariel. This is it. The Tempest you've—we've been waiting for. It's your enchanted island turning fiction into reality. Or are you dreading it now?'

'No, oh no . . .' she stammered. 'But you——'

'Me too, darling. God help me, I can't fight it any more.'

She closed her eyes, weak with dawning excitement, and hearing his low, unsteady groan, she opened her eyes again to catch the unguarded hunger in his dark gaze. And they smiled at each other, in a silent unbarred understanding.

For a moment she thought he meant to pick her up in his arms, but he obviously thought better of it, as with a slight push, he made her turn around and face the kitchen door. 'Come on, you. Better lead the way. You know the house better than me.' He picked up the kerosene lamp as he spoke.

She led the way straight to his bedroom, not bothering to ask for his approval. Somehow she couldn't see Kane's forceful presence against the girlish frills of her own childhood room. The sight of his bed, still ruffled, and the pillow still bearing the mark of his head, increased her panicked anticipation to an almost unbearable pitch. In mild surprise she realised that the furious sounds of the wind and rain outside were reduced to a dull, distant hum, deadened by the inner roar of her pounding pulse.

He was one step behind her, and she could hear him softly shutting the door. An invisible hand pulled the blanket which she was holding loosely around her.

'Turn around, Ariel,' he said quietly.

She did and made a step towards him, shaking with excitement and inexplicable fear.

'No, stay there. I want to look at you. We have all the time in the world now . . . and I intend to drag every second to the limit. No, don't cover yourself, darling. Here, give me your hands.'

He put the lamp on the floor and grabbed her nervous hands, his arms rigidly stretched to their full length, forcing her to keep her distance, as his eyes roamed unhurried and deliberate over her body which glinted dully in the dim lamplight.

'You're beautiful, you know?' he commented finally, almost impersonally. 'My senses tell me I must have seen a few women in my time, though for the life of me I can't remember any single one of them. Yet I do know that you take my breath away with your loveliness. I know I want you . . . God, I want you so badly, it hurts.'

Bending his elbows, he at last pulled her to him, marvelling at the fragility of her delicate bones against his hard body, his hands immediately rising to push through her long hair, both palms tightening against the sides of her face, as his eyes now limited their voracious roving from her mouth to her eyes which were hypnotised by his hard, unsmiling lips, and back to her mouth which now half opened in anticipation of his kiss.

He didn't kiss her. Instead, he bent down slightly to pick her up in his arms, and strode over to the bed, to lower her down on the rumpled sheets. With the same deliberate unhurried movements, he went back to pick up the kerosene lamp and put it on the low bedside table.

'I want to see your face when I love you, Ariel,' he explained, in the same strangely detached, tight voice. 'Here, let me pull that blanket from under you.'

Her head now empty of all thoughts, she slightly arched her body as he pulled the crumpled blanket, throwing it carelessly on the floor. Then, his eyes, forcing hers to remain on him, he deftly unbuckled the leather belt, unzipped his shabby jeans, and suddenly he was standing there, tall, upright, naked. She didn't realise that she was staring until she raised her eyes, and saw him smiling down at her, lovingly amused.

Again he held himself back, refusing to submit to the growing torment of his desire. He remained where he was, at the foot of the bed, looking down at her, his eyes sparing none of the secrets of her defenceless, naked body.

If she tried, she couldn't retreat behind the natural embarassment in face of that immobile, naked, totally exposed intimacy of their locked gaze, the kind of soul-baring intimacy which is made bearable only by touch, by the blind frenzy of a sensual embrace.

Her eyes came down finally, unable to take much more of that exquisite torture of self-exposure. She heard a faint rustle and her nostrils flared with his intoxicating male smell, as she sensed the warmth of his naked body stretched now alongside her on the bed, still untouching.

At last his hands moved towards her body, and started their slow reacquaintance with the smooth skin, the slim curves he had only once allowed himself to savour, slow and secure now without the restricting barriers of clothes. She could feel his breath whispering against her cheeks as his head came nearer, to cover her face with light, airy kisses, his mouth moving from her closed eyes, to her forehead, even her small, short nose, leaving her lips to the very last. But once there, he abandoned the gentle teasing and hungrily captured her mouth in his, his tongue invading her with the unleashed thirst of his need.

She cried when he tore himself away, her hands clinging to his withdrawing shoulders.

'Don't hurry me, darling. Give me time to love you.' The words were almost muffled as he buried his hungry mouth in her skin, tracing a hot, moist line down her slim, long neck, descending on her small firm breast. His tongue circled the aching nipple, teasing it to rigidity, and when he heard her groan with sweet agony, his hand came up, the long soothing fingers groping for her mouth, which hungrily closed around them, imitating his play with her nipple, unconscious of the suggestive sensuality of its abandoned greed.

And then she stiffened as his free hand began its gentle exploration of her most vulnerable self. Shocked by the unbearably sweet intimacy of the touch, her teeth closed involuntarily in a vicious bite on the fingers which were still captured in her mouth. The bitten hand was withdrawn, but the other persisted with its teasing play soon making her body quiver with delicious response.

And then both hands suddenly took a firm, tight hold of her shivering thighs, pinning them to the bed, and her breasts were suddenly left exposed to the chilly air as his whole body slid further down.

Later, she almost regretted that he had intoxicated her with so much excruciating pleasure. When she was less overwhelmed by the utter newness of it all, she was able to savour every subtle sensation, glory both physically and mentally in every variety of sensual gratification he kept coming up with. But this time, her first time, drowning as she was in the mindless, terrifying whirlpool of sensual discovery, she was too assailed by her body's exquisite responses to the unfamiliar sensations to relish the full enchantment of her pleasure.

She was senselessly drugged by it now. She had no mind, no body as she yielded to the inevitable ultimate bliss, striving for it yet at the same time gripped by a dark terror of being destroyed by the force of that unknown sensual fulfilment. She was so lost to reality that she was no longer conscious even of the man who was doing all this to her. Her hands were resting listlessly on the hard shoulders, insensible of Kane's escalating hunger as he kept up his relentless loving, patiently denying his body its own gratification, deriving his sole pleasure from the intent, deliberate manipulation of her own fulfilment.

When it happened, it didn't explode with a shattering finality. It came slowly, gently, with incredible sweetness. She felt light as air, washed by wave after wave of delicious joy, to dissolve finally in creamy contentment.

He heard her low moan, felt the uncontrollable quivering of her body and only then, he moved away. When her arms came up, groping for him in blind panic, as if gripped by fear of being abandoned, he chuckled softly. She opened her eyes, searching frantically for his withdrawn body, and she met his blue smiling gaze, right above her.

She felt safe, utterly content, flowing with heady love. 'I don't think I could bear going through it again,' she said gravely, looking wonderingly into his smiling eyes. 'Is it always like this?'

'I really wouldn't know, kitten. The fact is that I'm quite mystified myself. I mean, after all, I'm just as virginal as you are.' He grinned at her perplexed expression. 'In this life, darling, you're my first woman. Or rather, you soon will be.'

Her throaty chuckle was breathless with the wonder of it as she snuggled into the hard, pulsating wall of his body which now descended to cover hers wholly. His arms came under her back to scoop her content body to him, no longer patient, and his mouth found her swollen, soft lips, hurting them with almost angry kisses.

She moaned as that drowsy need began to stir her body again, responding to the hungry pull of his knowing, aroused body and the hard demand of his roaming hands. His back was arched as he lay above her, so that she could see his face and chest which glinted dully in the gloomy light of the kerosene lamp and she forced her heavy eyes to stay open, so that she could glory in her effect on him as she watched the smiling lips tighten and the amused, glinting gaze darken with the intensity of his desire.

He made no effort to free himself from the hold of her steady stare, and she was the first to yield, her eyes shutting automatically, overwhelmed by the thrilling touch as his muscular thigh pushed her legs apart.

'No, Ariel, don't.' His voice was husky, almost harsh. 'Keep your eyes open, darling.'

She did so, reluctantly drifting back from the new engulfing waves of sensuality. His eyes were drowning hers in their dark depth as he moved with short, hardly noticeable pushes, withdrawing slightly and again pushing in, tormenting her with teasing gentleness after the storm of passion he had taught her before.

'Now, my love.' He sounded almost desperate. 'Look at me!'

His eyes were attempting to anaesthetise her to the coming pain as in one sudden, powerful thrust, he was inside her, and she choked a cry.

'Oh God, I love you, Ariel!' he gasped, and she knew by the intensity, the force of words that he had just given her his oath. And she smiled through her tears, in response. 'I love you, Kane.'

With a stifled moan, his mouth descended to cover her smiling lips in a deep kiss. Then he remained still, utterly motionless, inside her sore body.

'Don't move,' he ordered when she tried to stroke the skin of his back, damp with perspiration. 'Just lie still, my love. I'm here, with you.'

They lay like that, still and unmoving, waiting for her taut body to relax as the pain grew fainter and finally faded away. And once again, holding her head with both hands, he began to rock against her, cautiously at first, and then, when her face remained lax and clear, he increased the pace, penetrating deeper and deeper with each thrust.

Her body, totally, magically in harmony with his, was moving to meet his slow, insistent, rhythmic thrusts. Her arms were no longer stroking, but grasping, demanding, moving down to the small of his back, as if to increase the force of his motion. She felt no fear, no terror of the unknown because she trusted him so completely though she had no idea where he was taking her. He had no face, no name, no identity. She was no longer a separate body, but a part of him. She wasn't aware that he tore his mouth away from hers, her whole being steeped in that hypnotic rocking motion in which they were both soaring higher and higher, towards a mysterious, ever-nearing ultimate end and then she was flooded with the total knowledge of the mystery as their minds and bodies merged in the eruption of their union.

She heard his shuddered groan mingled with her own sharp, clear cry, before she sank into a peaceful well of bliss.

'Don't go away,' she murmured, when in her deep, dark daze she felt him move above her.

'Go away?' he chuckled, his breathing still uneven. 'You must be joking.' And he rolled off her to lie on his back, drawing her to him, so that her head was now resting on his damp chest, close enough to hear the mad race of his throbbing heart. She tried to calm it down with her light kisses.

His arm tightened its hold on her head, pressing it closer to his heart. 'Go to sleep now, Ariel,' he murmured, his voice heavy with drowsy contentment. 'And in case you didn't hear me before,' she could hear him mumble as he drifted off into a deep sleep, 'I love you.'

She was vaguely astonished to note that the dim bedroom was still shaking and shuddering under the angry lashing of the whirling wind outside. She had totally forgotten about the gale.

They woke up together, their eyes meeting with sleepy blankness and instantly warming up with a smiling welcome. The room, usually washed in the bright light of the morning sun, was dark and gloomy, to remind them of the stormy night behind them.

'It's over,' they said in unison and laughed, as Kane scooped her to his warm chest, and gave her forehead a light kiss.

'How do you feel?'

She managed to copy his light, casual tone: 'Nice. And you?'

'Even more so!' he said. 'Want to check the damage outside first?'

'First to what?' she asked, puzzled. 'Breakfast?'

'No, not exactly.' He suddenly pulled her on top of him, laughingly crashing her fragile frame against his. 'First to this . . . but don't bother to answer. You've lost your chance to put in your vote.'

They made love again, unhurried, sleepily, delighted and amused by each other's inventive waywardness, no longer driven by the intensity of their first union.

It was eight when they finally got up, showered together, and went down to meet the world. Ariel made straight to the telephone, to call the hospital for news of her mother.

'The telephone's dead,' she announced, her voice reaching the kitchen where Kane was already pottering with the breakfast things.

'So is the generator,' he called back. 'No electricity. Long live the Aga stove!'

Their clothes were still lying on the floor, to remind them, if they needed a reminder, of the events which preceded their first night together. And Ariel carelessly threw them into the laundry basket.

'You're used to servants, aren't you?' he asked casually.

'I can manage perfectly well without them, if that's what you're driving at. If you think lack of money could put me off you, you're wasting your irony. Besides, you're going to make millions with your book.'

She regretted her words before she finished the sentence. His smile faded and he was looking at her with a curious mixture of exasperation and something like regret. 'Eat your melon, Ariel, and shut up,' he said finally, quite mildly.

The damage was done, though. The memory of his angry threat was now clouding her perfect blue horizon.

The sun was shining brightly on the muddy mess which the gale left behind. But on the whole it did little damage. The islanders, used to the unpredictable moods of the Indian Ocean climate, were quite immune to the dirt and disorder. Things could be far worse, like the demolition of their homes, even loss of life.

The beach shed was gone, its beams buried under the palm-leaf roof, but their typewriters, protected by their cases, were undamaged. Even the flimsy cabinet was still there, in broken bits of sodden plywood. Mercifully, it held nothing but stationery and a supply of typing paper. The pitiful condition of the blank pages certainly justified both her and Kane's foray into the storm the night before to salvage the only copy of their respective manuscripts.

She breathed in relief when they reached the bay

and found *Laura*, the Stewarts' yacht, rolling
peacefully on the calm water, still safely secured to her
mooring. 'Twice in the past she drifted out to sea,
during gentler storms than the one we had last night.'
Ariel explained her sigh of relief. 'Come on, let's call
the hospital on the radio.'

Julian Stewart's metallic voice came in shortly,
hiding his concern and worry under dry, irritable
scolding. 'About time too . . . I've been trying to get
the house since six o'clock.'

'The phone is dead, Daddy, and we overslept, I'm
afraid. How's Mummy?' Laura Stewart was fine, her
father assured her, but there was little chance of their
returning home before the end of the week. No
transportation. Unlike St Patrick, Mahe was badly hit
by the gale, and everything was at sixes and sevens.
'What's the damage, besides the phone lines?' he asked
carefully.

She knew what he really wanted to hear. 'I'm fine,
Dad. So is Kane. The house hasn't been touched. The
generator has packed up, but we'll manage, Dad.
Don't worry. Just give Mum my love.'

'I will. And tell Kane I appreciate his help. I feel
much better knowing that he's there, looking after
you. Bye now.'

The stillness in the cabin was disturbed only by the
soft hum of the ocean. Kane was standing behind her,
his silence saying more than any words. Angrily, she
whirled around to face him. 'Don't look at me like
that, Kane. This is silly. You are looking after me . . .
I mean, last night, I could have been blown away in
that gale and you——'

'Shut up, Ariel,' he said quietly and walked briskly
away from her, making his way to the deck.

She followed him. 'You're not going to . . . You're
not thinking of what you said the other night, about
leaving here if anything happened between us, are
you?' she rushed on, frightened by his silence.

He was standing by the railings, looking out to the
misty islands in the blue horizon, his rigid, bare back
shutting her off.

'You can't, Kane . . . You can't go! Not now!'

The stiff muscles of his shoulders slackened, and at last he turned back to face her. She breathed again; his face was once again open and giving. 'Don't think about it, Ariel. Now, what's the usual procedure on St Patrick after a bad storm?'

She had no other option but obey his command to the letter. For the rest of their time together, she resolutely banished any thoughts of the future, any anxiety or thoughts of doom from her mind.

That morning, when they returned to the house, they found Marie and Jacques already hard at work, clearing the debris and settling back into the daily routine of the Stewart household. Neither Kane nor she felt inclined to share their new intimacy with others. Work was out of the question; their minds were too raw with memories of the night before and too preoccupied with the next, to leave any space for the novel or its adaptation. So they spent the day patching up the palm-thatched shed, and clearing the mess. Then, waiting for the minute Marie and Jacques returned to their own families, they swam, skin-dived and wandered around the island, cautiously avoiding any touch which might end up with an uncontrollable surge of desire.

They were less cautious the days after. After another long, sleepless night of love, they no longer shunned the hospitality of the small, barely inhabited island which offered numerous isolated and enchantingly beautiful substitutes to the enclosure of Kane's bedroom. It was useless, if not downright impossible, to keep apart whenever they felt like loving again, which was practically every moment of the day.

These were the most glorious days of her life, and precisely because of that, they utterly ruined her for any other life afterwards.

As Kane had warned her, the first night was only an introduction to the secret treasure of delights contained within their bodies. With his utterly uninhibited sensuality, and warm, humorous nature, Kane was set to expose the mysteries of their bodies, leading her into the secret treasure of her own sensuality with a sure, loving hand. Ariel, in spite of natural, uncomplicated spontaneity, did recoil from time to time, shocked or embarrassed by the force of her passion, incredulous at her own shameless abandon. But his amused, warm laughter and delighted encouragement wiped out any remnants of inhibitions in her. As he said to her one moonless night, while they were swimming naked in the warm water of the bay: 'We're pretty amazing, you know, considering the fact that we were both uninitiated, one way or another. I guess other people take years to cover the ground we have done in a few days.'

He was as generous with his love as he was with his body, yet never maudlin, never stickily romantic, letting his eyes, his lips his hands demonstrate his feelings, and replacing the trite words of love with wry, perceptive and always unshakably frank retorts. Ariel wasn't a fairy-tale sprite any more than he was Prince Charming. They were just a man and a woman, 'with a healthy—all right, rather more than just healthy appetite for each other.'

'And that's all?' she asked, mildly. She wasn't very much given to flowery speeches either.

'Well, I guess the gods of St Patrick did show some sense in sending you someone like me. It's almost the perfect match, don't you think? I mean, they could have picked any poor bloke who happened to be drowning in the vicinity, couldn't they? And where would you be then? Or I, for that matter?'

'I know where you would be,' she answered, mocking his unabashed smugness. 'Probably going through the umpteenth session with some stodgy psychiatrist, struggling to solve the mystery of your past, or back with your sympathetic and totally puzzled family, trying to fill you up on all the missing gaps in your memory.'

'God forbid,' he breathed, in mock horror. Neither needed to say aloud the thought that occurred to both of them at the same time: it may still happen, though. And probably very soon.

The night before Laura and Julian returned home, Ariel could no longer hold back the gnawing anxiety. It was almost dawn, and their lovemaking had been explosive with Ariel drowning in total abandonment, and Kane, with an amused anticipation, allowing her to take control. His loud, unguarded cry of fulfilment left her weak not only with her own mind-blowing peak but with a sense of feminine triumph.

Pulling her down, Kane turned her around, her back to him, and curled her against his long frame, one arm around her waist, the other cupping her breast, settling spoon-fashion for sleep.

'Kane,' she said into the gloomy chill of early dawn. 'What about tomorrow?'

'You mean, today, don't you?'

'You know exactly what I mean. What happens when they come back?'

'How about we go back to work?' he suggested, mildly.

'Please, Kane. Answer me . . .'

He didn't speak for a long moment. 'I don't know, kitten,' he said finally. 'Let's just make it up as we go along, shall we?'

To her surprise, they adjusted instantly to the inevitable change in their life upon her parents' return. They actually did go back to work and to their various vigorous sports, and kept their passion under firm leash. Even Ariel couldn't face making love in secret, betraying her parents' trust in Kane.

But the feeling of approaching doom was now with Ariel permanently. It was with immense relief that she saw him at the breakfast table every morning, as if she had expected him to vanish during the night. He said nothing about his plans, nor showed any outward signs of having reached a decision, but she knew it was coming, and was helpless to do anything to prevent it.

It was about ten days after her parents' return. They were working in the beach shed, back to back as usual, their two typewriters competing with each other in furious rattle.

Suddenly his typewriter went silent. 'How are you

feeling, Ariel?' He spoke into the air, not turning to her.

'Fine, thank you,' she said, mockingly polite.

She gasped when she heard his next words, suddenly understanding his drift. 'Any signs of a baby on the way?' As always, he was drastically direct.

For a second, she was tempted to say yes. At least, she thought desperately, she could detain him for a few more weeks. But she knew that even if she could bring herself to lie, he would see through her in a minute.

'No,' she said finally, drily. 'No such luck!'

'Right.' He turned at last to face her, grinning. 'So that's at least one bridge we've managed to cross.'

Her voice sounded strange even to her, low and tight and hard, 'Will you tell me before you leave?'

'No,' he said softly. 'I'm sorry, darling. I don't think I could face it.'

'I'll say goodbye now, then.'

'Goodbye, Ariel.'

He was behind her suddenly, his hands coming down on her shoulders in a painful grip. Almost violently, he pulled her up and turned her to him to bury her tear-stained face against his chest. They didn't kiss, only clung to each other for a timeless desperate moment, in utter silence. Then, cupping her face with his hands, his fingers ploughing into her long glistening tresses, he made her raise her head to meet the depth of his dark blue gaze, as if trying to brand her image on his mind.

The raw pain she saw in his eyes wrenched her heart, and she smiled, trying to comfort him, forgetting her own misery for a second. And at last, he answered with his crooked, well-loved grin. Then, planting a light kiss on the top of her head, he let her go.

And they turned back to their typewriters.

Next day, she was having her usual early morning swim, a fair distance from the beach, when she saw the small two-seater plane land on the landing strip, below their house. And all her hardened resolution melted away, as she made for the shore, her usual powerful stroke clumsy and slow, handicapped by her frantic need to speak to him, touch him once more. When she finally reached the shore, the little plane was already taxiing along, about to take off. Through the window, she saw the dark outline of Kane's proud profile. He had only to turn his head to see her standing, knee-deep in the water, frozen into immobility. But he kept his gaze stiffly ahead. And then he was gone.

She had found out later that day that Kane had spoken to her parents on the very day they had come back from Mahe. He had been almost brutal in his determination to be utterly frank with them.

Naturally, they weren't surprised to hear of his love for their daughter, and for all their strict values and morals, could hardly blame him or Ariel for succumbing under the circumstances. Their shock came when it finally dawned on them that there could be no question of a wedding.

'He did nothing to spare us or himself, Ariel.' Laura's voice was aching with sympathy for her daughter. 'He told us the truth about his being here in St Patrick, about his loss of memory. He's a man without a past, without identity, Ariel,' she went on, justifying his reasoning. 'He had no right to tie you to him.'

'You mean, you and Daddy encouraged him to leave?'

'No, we didn't,' her father now broke in, his tight control over his emotions making him sound angry and gruff, 'I didn't need any references or background information to form an opinion about him. I know a good man when I see one.'

'Your father suggested he stayed on the island, and started a new life here, with you. But he wouldn't hear of it. He said he'd have to find out who he was before he could accept our trust in him. And he was right, Ariel,' Laura went on, firmly. 'You'll have to wait until he comes back, fully recovered, or . . .'

'Or learn to live without him.' Ariel supplied the

rest of the sentence. 'I know. I've heard him say the same thing over and over again. Well, I can't do much else, can I? I wasn't asked, or even consulted. You, Kane, everyone very cautiously and sensibly considered my future, my life, my well-being . . . but none of you considered my feelings. I'm young, my whole life is before me, and I'll get over it, right?'

Her parents stared silently, at this new, hard, bitter woman to whom they had given life.

'Well, I may be young, and my life as you say is still before me, but I'll never, never get over Kane. I'll have no other man. So you'd better tell him that next time you see him.'

There was no next time, though. In spite of his promise to keep her parents informed of his whereabouts, he never phoned or wrote. So her parents said, at least. She suspected them of hiding the truth from her, to protect her perhaps.

Mercifully, self-preservation instincts had blurred Ariel's memory of the following days, weeks, months.

She had never known pain before. People, both family and strangers, succumbed almost instantly to her sprightly spontaneity, her affectionate nature. She had never met with real hostility or rejection. So she had no defences, no means of protection against the perpetual, relentless pain of loss forever sharpened by the vivid memories associated with every corner of the island, every daily activity, every sound and smell. Everything, in fact, which she had shared with Kane. She was eaten up by the rawness of the pain, robbed even of the sour comfort of anger or resentment for the man who was the cause of it. She knew that he was aching for her as much as she was for him, and the knowledge only added to her suffering.

Six months passed by, Christmas was on them again, marking a year since Kane had been washed ashore on the island, and yet the pain was still as sharp, cruel, soul-destroying as ever.

And it was then that Michael came for his annual holiday and told her about Chris Donahue.

She hadn't touched her adaptation of Kane's novel

since his departure. Once she had realised he had taken the only copy of his unfinished work with him, she lost all interest in her own work. But just before leaving St Patrick for England, she went down to the shed and took the thick file out, intending to use it as a proof of their past relations. Her only tangible proof, in fact. And it was then that she found his farewell note, resting on top of the typed pages.

I won't ask you to forget me, Ariel, as we both know you won't. Just remember whenever you think of me: no matter how treacherous my memory has been in the past, it'll always remain faithful to you. My heart tells me that I have never loved anyone as I love you and my whole being shouts out that I shall never love anyone else. So, my love, till we meet again, Kane.

CHAPTER SIX

A KNIFE-SHARP pang of yearning jerked Ariel out of the past back into the hopeless mess of her present situation.

It seemed hard to believe that only yesterday she was ready to give her right arm for the chance of spending a few days in Chris Donahue's company. Right now, having had a foretaste of what threatened to be a set pattern in their working relationship, she wished she had never talked herself into that impossible charade. She had thought then that the pain she had experienced after Kane's departure had immunised her to anything. But she hadn't bargained for the relentless, superhuman effort she had to exercise over her mind as well as her senses. This was beyond her powers.

Her mind was made up.

It was past midnight, too late to call Paul Andrews. But she would call him first thing in the morning, she

determined, and ask him to find someone else and free
her from this hell. No matter how short her trial
period proved to be, she simply couldn't go on with
this ordeal a day longer.

It seemed possible, even easy, while Chris Donahue,
the writer, was dominant. She could control the
perpetual surge of memories and yearnings which the
mere sight of him aroused in her, as long as the man
himself kept rejecting her with that indifferent
arrogance and cold distrust. He looked like Kane,
obviously retained Kane's virile power over her
senses, and like Kane, overwhelmed her by his sharp
intelligence and extraordinary talent. But her obstinate,
unshaken love for Kane had been nurtured by that
wonderful combination of warmth, inner strength,
self-knowledge and tenderness which were uniquely
Kane's. Devoid of these qualities, Chris could win her
admiration for his talent and brains, he could even
make her body ache for him with his devastating virile
attraction, but he could have very little power over her
heart.

But during that first day, she had seen Chris
Donahue's gradual transformation into the man she
once knew. Secure in the camaraderie of their work,
succumbing to the old affinity between them, he was
slowly shedding that hard protective skin to reveal the
nature which was truly his, whether in his present life
or in the lost, forgotten one.

It was like falling in love all over again. Yet her
chances of finding happiness in this new love were
practically nil.

She had no doubt that she could make him want
her. Over the last three years she had had enough
proof of the effect she had on men. She never asked
for it, and never really understood it, but she would
have been blind to ignore the fact. It hadn't bothered
her too much because she had always managed to
intercept those first undeniable signs and turn the
would-be seducer into a good, loyal friend. And she
never felt the slightest temptation to respond to any of
them.

But with Chris, she knew she would be powerless to resist him. How could she, when she had already known his love, had shared with him such depths of intimacy, such heights of ecstatic pleasure?

Why not then? she asked herself, angrily. Why not take what was there? Perhaps, through his body, she could reach his soul as well. Perhaps she had already begun to stir it . . .

With desperate eagerness, she tried to kindle the weak flame of hope: Chris Donahue did respond to her. He was deeply shaken by the sound of her laughter, admitting freely that he had been haunted by it. And today . . . that almost ethereal moment, when Kane's words erupted from the dark grave of his lost memory, without him even realising he had spoken them.

Was it possible that by staying near him, gently prodding his memory, she could bring Kane back to life again?

She could tell him the truth, she thought, with growing conviction. Unveil the mystery of the black hole which was making his present life so barren and hollow. He was obviously a driven, unhappy man, shutting himself away from the world, protecting himself by that unnatural arrogant aloofness from any involvement.

Yes, she had the power to put an end to his troubles with a few words, and yet . . .

And yet that was no guarantee that he, as Chris, would love her as Kane had done when he was a lonely, lost amnesiac. Her ears were ringing with the echo of the painful words that he had flung at her that night in the shed, when he warned her off him with such cold fury: 'If you can trust the feelings of a man who has no past or future, only a present that consists of a half-finished fictitious fantasy, an enchanted island and the female version of Shakespeare's Ariel, then yes, I love you.'

She was almost certain that he would take her back, once he knew the truth. Out of gratitude or a sense of obligation for what she had once been to him. Kane had sacrificed his love for her because of a ridiculous sense of responsibility, chivalry, fairness, call it what you will. Chris was just as capable of sacrificing his new self and taking her back without love, for exactly the same reasons. This was something she could never accept. She wanted his love, not his integrity.

By two o'clock she was still awake, her head bursting with the same thoughts going round and round, her tired body battered to death by the tension of self-control imposed on it for so many hours. She hadn't even taken off her clothes yet.

It was hopeless.

She would do better to use the sleepless hours and process another scene from her old adaptation and have it ready for next day, when they would start working in earnest on the script. He didn't seem to mind her showing some initiative, and she was certain he would approve of most of it, since he himself had been closely involved with its conception.

She managed to find her way to the study quite easily. She or Chris must have left on the lights when they left it, because a thin beam guided her across the spacious lounge towards its door. Still unsuspicious, she walked in, noting that the room was lit only by the dimmed spotlight above the Eames chair.

Only when she reached the desk, her heart began to pound uncomfortably.

She knew something was terribly wrong the moment she saw the open drawer. She had carefully kept it shut and locked throughout the day. And for a very good reason. The last thing she wanted was for Chris to notice the thin binder in which she kept the first few scenes of the script adaptation from his St Patrick days.

The binder was gone.

She was hardly surprised when a bodiless voice reached her from the deep Eames chair. 'If you're looking for your script, I've got it here. And I'm impressed. Deeply.'

He remained seated, hidden behind the deep curve of the lounger. Only his long legs were visible, resting on the matching stool, in that characteristically relaxed, lazy grace.

'You obviously share my aversion to sleep. So by all means, let's go on working. Do you mind coming closer?'

When she didn't respond, he swung the lounger in one swift move, and faced her from across the room, the soft light making his blue eyes glint in that frightening cold fury she had known only once before. 'I said, come closer!'

Like that computerised humanoid in his novel, she found herself walking slowly to his side.

'Sit down, over there, on the stool.'

When she hesitated, his hand shot out and pulled her down, cruelly. 'Now,' he said softly, freezing her with his controlled rage. 'Let's take it piece by piece. You were offered the job a little more than twenty-four hours ago. Assuming you were confident enough of trapping me, you still couldn't have known about the film project before my meeting with producers which had taken place less than a week ago. So how did you manage to produce almost a quarter of the novel, broken into tidy episodes, properly formated, including full dialogues, and all the trimmings?' He hardly raised his voice when she remained silent. 'Answer me, Ariel.'

'I . . .' Her mind was churning crazily, trying to come up with an adequate lie. 'I had your manuscript for over a month. I got it from your . . . Paul gave it to me.'

'Come off it, darling. This manuscript has been kept under tight security. Paul is the first one to be wary of pirates. So what's the true story?'

'My . . . one of the junior agents there is a close friend and he got me a copy.' She was already thinking of a fictitious name for the traitor. But Chris wasn't interested right now.

'So, you have cold-bloodedly coerced some poor bastard into a criminal act which, if he is lucky, would only put an end to his career. Why? What the hell was so important about getting hold of my novel?'

Her imagination could go no further. She just looked at him, helplessly.

'Was it the novel?' He went on grilling her mercilessly. 'Or was it what I've suspected from the very first time I laid eyes on you. You were after me, am I getting warm?'

It seemed the only possible answer right now. She nodded, weakly.

'I see ... So at least we've got that far. All right, then, let's hear it. What is it about me that you find important enough to go to such lengths? My money? My name? Or just a simple fascination with my virile charms?'

The last words broke through her guilty meekness. 'You bastard,' she spat at him, 'you cold, arrogant bastard!'

'Bastard, yes ... even arrogant, if you insist. But at least I've got some pride, which is more than you can say for yourself.'

All her misery, her tormented doubts and raw emotions, burst out now in a fit of rage she had never believed herself capable of. Her clenched fists flew at him, raining pathetically ineffective blows on his hard, unyielding chest. He let her vent her fury for a second, then with contemptuous ease, he trapped both frantic fists in one hand, and pulled her down on top of his reclining body.

'Oh, no!' That was what she had been terrified of all along. The tangible, physical contact with his body, the feel of his hard pulsating chest, his hands, his muscled thighs, the invasion of his familiar, intoxicating smell. And his clean-shaven face, so dangerously near now, no more than a hazy blur, robbing her of her sole protection against the memory of Kane's bearded one. 'Oh please, don't!' Her cry ended in a broken sob.

He let go of her defeated hands, and caught her face between his two palms, his long fingers ploughing into her short hair, tightening their grip on her head, and pulling it down to meet his unloving, disdainful lips, in a closed mouth, cruel kiss which ground her tender lips against her teeth, until she could taste the blood.

The pain inflicted by the crush of his cruel mouth was her salvation.

He was as different from Kane as any of the other men who had tried to force themselves on her, trying to arouse her senses with loveless, undiscriminating desire. And like them, he left her cold. She remained motionless for a few seconds, refusing to gratify him with any show of resistance, and felt a glow of angry satisfaction when he finally let her go, pushing her head away with a grunt of disgust.

He made no attempt to hold her down when she pulled away to regain her seat on the stool.

'Well, was it worth the trouble?' he asked drily, watching her wipe her hand across her mouth, in an unconscious gesture of distaste. They were both completely calm now, and icy cold.

'Let me see if I can answer your question point by point,' she said, her voice dead quiet. 'As for your money, my father has enough to keep me and my brother in luxury even if we weren't making quite a respectable living for ourselves. As for your name, well, frankly, I'd rather be famous for myself than for the man who deigned to take me to his bed. And as for your virile charms . . .' The words were coming out now in a furious torrent. 'You've been very careful to keep them stashed away, evidently with the very commendable intention of protecting panting hot females like me from temptation. You can't really believe that I'd go to all the trouble of acquiring your manuscript, slave over its adaptation, just because of what I imagined you might look like?'

She stopped, out of breath, to gulp some air into her lungs. Only now she realised that he was shaking with laughter.

'Good Heavens, you never faltered! Not once throughout the whole speech. You should put yourself up for Prime Minister,' he said finally, in between chuckles.

She waited, her face grave, till he became serious

again and then went on, coolly, remorselessly, lying her head off. 'I'll tell you why I was so determined to get your book, and to work with you. I wanted to work on the adaptation. It could do a hell of a lot for my career.'

'As a secretary?'

'I'm not a secretary.' She opted for part of the truth as the best way out now. 'I'm a script-writer.'

She thought she detected a hint of disappointment, as if he had lost whatever little interest he had in her. He obviously considered ruthless ambition rather trite. 'You mean, you were under the illusion that working with me would have catapulted you into the tightly guarded world of professional script-writing?'

'No, that's not what I mean at all. I am a professional writer already, with nine scripts to my name. Commissioned and produced too! Afternoon serials, as well as a few drama episodes. I just wanted to get a credit in a major novel adaptation. It pays well, and its more prestigious than soaps. I wanted to have something ready so I could get in on the act before anyone else could beat me to it. I had no way of knowing that you would insist on doing the adaptation yourself, had I?' She was falling into the old trap of babbling away in case the well of her overflowing imagination would dry half way. 'So I asked Paul to get me the job with you. I was quite prepared to be demoted to the rank of assistant, or ghost-writer, if I could later on use my experience for a proper piece of adaptation . . . I mean, with my name on it——'

Her voice trailed away, fading into silence, as she suddenly registered the old haunted look take hold of his face. It was happening again, like the day before when he heard her laugh, or this afternoon, when he watched her devour her sandwich. It was eerie, terrifying, as if she was assisting in a medium trance.

'What is it?' she asked, her heart wrenched in sympathy.

He was staring at her, his wide-open eyes dark with angry, tortured bewilderment. 'Ariel . . .' He pronounced her name almost vehemently. 'Your name *is*

Ariel, I take it. You haven't just assumed it as part of your plan to get to me, have you?'

'No, I haven't. It's always been Ariel.'

He wasn't listening to her. 'Ariel . . . Ariel?' He kept repeating the name again and again. 'Ariel . . .' And then, his hands came up to cover his face, and she heard him groan. 'It's so damn near . . . Why the hell can't I reach it!'

Her eyes were brimming with tears now. She had witnessed Kane going through the same torture so many times, while she could only look on helplessly, unable to do anything to ease it.

'Oh, please, Kane. Stop tormenting yourself . . .'

The name slipped out of her unguarded lips so naturally, that it took her a second before she realised what she had just done.

She watched him as he slowly raised his head and with an effort focused on his dark, fathomless eyes on her.

'What did you call me?'

It was too late now to turn back. 'Kane,' she said clearly. 'I called you Kane.'

His eyes held hers for an endless, intolerable moment. They showed no hint of dawning recollection, not even a glint of suspicion. And then, his voice quite normal, he asked, 'Who is Kane?'

Ariel felt the blood beginning to flow again through her veins. Strangely, she felt relieved, as if they had both just had a narrow escape.

'Oh, he's . . . a friend,' she stammered.

'The junior agent, is it?'

'The junior agent?' it took her a second to grasp that he was referring to her fictitious accessory. 'Oh, no. Certainly not him. Kane is . . . was someone rather special.' She ended weakly.

'Was?'

'Yes . . .'

'Is he dead?'

She hesitated, tempted to lie but somehow held back by some odd superstition. 'No, he's just . . . gone.'

His voice remained deliberately cool and dry, but she detected the sympathy behind it. 'And you loved him . . .'

She nodded silently, her eyes averted.

'You still do, I take it. Shall we talk about him?'

Her large eyes fixed on him for a fraction of a second, their expression for once as unfathomable as his. 'No,' she said tiredly. 'I don't think I can. Not yet.'

'Oh, I see . . .' Gravely, he studied her drained, expressionless face. 'So I'm on trial too, am I?'

'Pardon?'

'I too have to prove that I deserve your trust,' he said quietly. 'That's what you were trying to tell me, wasn't it?'

Ariel stood up, reaching the end of her tether. 'You're wrong,' she said quietly, turning away from his shrewd eyes. 'You don't have to prove anything. You may have my trust any time, if you ever feel you want it.'

She didn't see the gentle expression which softened the hard handsome face. 'You'd better go to bed now, Ariel. Or you'll be no use to me in the morning. Don't forget. You have to process those four scenes into the computer before I resume my slave-driving at ten o'clock.'

His words sank slowly into her tired, numb consciousness. 'You mean, we're still on? I'm not fired?'

'Heavens, no. You're going to save me a hell of a lot of time with your first drafts. Besides, I can't afford to lose you. You're too good a script-writer.'

She was at the door when his voice came after her: 'Just for the record, Ariel, I've decided to be guided by your feminine instincts. I've exterminated Alexis the humanoid. She is now a real girl, flesh and blood, on the brink of womanhood. So we might even have a convincing love story.'

She stiffened. 'I never criticised the love story in your novel, I just said that——'

'It is pretty stilted, and we both know it. So, here's

your chance to justify Paul Andrews's trust in you. By all means, turn Alexis into a Miranda and let her find her Ferdinand . . .'

'What!' Once again she fell an easy prey to the next dart of Chris's cruelly playful memory.

'It smacks a mile off, love.' She heard Kane speaking through his mouth. 'You've obviously caught the echoes of *The Tempest* in my novel. I thought I covered my tracks pretty well, but you seem to have found me out. I won't insult you again with my suspicions, but it does seem a very odd coincidence that your name is Ariel.'

'Yes, isn't it?' she answered, drugged into frivolity by emotional and physical exhaustion. 'What's more, I was born and raised on an enchanted island. Just like the one in your novel. Now how is that for a coincidence?'

She was almost at the door, when his light voice arrested her, friendly and deceptively casual. 'Just a minute, Ariel.'

'Yes?' She turned around.

'I know we've been over that one before but let me ask it once more and never again, I promise.' He looked at her calmly, his eyes reassuring her that whatever her answer, he would accept it, as long as it was honest. 'Did you know me then?'

Ariel's hand rose to her stomach, as if to ward off a physical blow. 'Then? You mean when———'

'I mean, when I was my other self. When, as you suggested yesterday, I'd been wandering like a lost soul in hell. Did you know me then?'

She made her decision in a fraction of a second. 'No.' She spoke clearly, amazing herself by the genuine regret she had managed to convey. 'No, I didn't.'

His cool eyes held her in a close scrutiny for a surprisingly short time. 'You sound almost sorry,' he said softly. 'I wonder why . . .'

'Because I would have liked to be able to help you unravel the mystery of that lost period. And because———' She hesitated.

'Yes, go on!'

'Because I think you could have done with a good friend then,' she ended firmly and left him without a further word.

She didn't call Paul Andrews next morning. In fact, she totally forgot that she had decided to ask him to relieve her of her impossible situation. That nocturnal encounter with Chris wiped her mind clean of all her sensible resolutions. Whatever the cost, whatever the pain, she was determined to stay on and make herself so indispensable to Chris Donahue that he wouldn't have the nerve to leave her behind when he took off for his haven in the Seychelles.

CHAPTER SEVEN

A MILD sunny afternoon heralded a break from the dull, drizzly weather they'd had all week. A gentle breeze blew in through the wide picture windows, filling the quiet study with chirpy sounds of birds and with cool fresh smells of the budding spring.

It was Saturday but that would hardly make any difference to Chris, she thought wryly. He would expect her to carry on working throughout the weekend, just as they had done the weekend before. Chris Donahue was a compulsive worker and had no concept of time at all. All he wanted was to get the adaptation over and done with so that he could get on with his next obsession and, she smiled ruefully to herself, be free of her company.

They had been together now for almost two weeks and as far as she could tell, Chris seemed quite pleased with his decision to employ her. After that nerve-racking beginning, they had settled into a harmonious, and at times even friendly, working relationship. Her original version was now used regularly as a first draft and there was no longer any question of her acting as a dumb, technical assistant. Chris always had the last word, naturally, but time and time again he would agree to her suggestions, gracefully accepting her objections to any changes he had made in his old version, as he had done in the case of Alexis, the humanoid. In fact, they had become equal collaborators.

Not that she could now take her employment for granted, of course. She was still on trial, living on borrowed time, never knowing whether she'd still be there the next day. He kept his promise of that first night and stopped laying traps for her, trying to catch her off her guard with his unpredictable, unsettling questions but he made it quite obvious that he still didn't trust her. He was always on his guard against the slightest attempt on her part, however innocent, to impinge on the privacy which he cherished so jealously. And every now and again she would catch his cool, assessing eyes on her and the sardonic grin which bluntly warned her that he was not fooled for a moment. She was guilty until proven innocent.

But the odd thing was that now she was no longer tormented by his suspicions and his thinly disguised impatience to get rid of her. Over the last two weeks she had become quite used to being treated as an impersonal, sexless collaborator though clever, useful, and even talented, as Chris admitted quite freely since their truce on her first night at the house.

She hardly remembered now the doubts and agony she had experienced that night. When she thought how close she was to calling her agent and asking to be released from the job, she could only smile now. Nothing could have been better for her peace of mind than those two weeks of close collaboration with the man who had been haunting her for three long years.

Michael should be able to make something of this, she smiled to herself. She seemed to have discovered a new way to rid people of their obsessions. Turning the disease into the cure itself. Like using snake poison to counteract a snake bite. It was as if living in close proximity with Kane's other self, coupled with his total indifference to her as a woman, was beginning to exorcise the ghost of the past.

She was quite amazed to discover as early as her second day here that she could regard Chris Donahue with the same detached appreciation that he had for her. She found him a stimulating and often amusing man to work with, and at times, especially after a fruitful and ingenious session, she even felt a thrilling tingle of physical attraction for that handsome and brilliant man. But as far as her heart was concerned, she now felt almost safe.

It didn't even matter much whether he'd take her with him to finish the adaptation aboard his yacht in the Seychelles. She was quite reconciled to the idea of waking up one morning to be told by Marjorie that Chris had flown off to the Seychelles and would no longer need her services. She might feel slightly disappointed at not having been allowed to finish the job, but no more than that. In fact, she was rather looking forward to a new life, free from both Kane and Chris.

Living as she had done over three years, suspended between despair and hope of finding Kane again, she had never really taken advantage of her life in London and her budding career. Yet she had a friendly, vivacious nature with a normal appetite for the kind of things which can make life rather pleasant: friends, good fun, professional success. She wasn't at all averse to the idea of becoming famous and successful and making mounds and mounds of money. It would mean, first of all, leaving the gloomy Dulwich house she shared with her brother, and moving into a flat in town without having to ask her father for financial help. It would also mean a rich, exciting social life, with lots of new friends and probably a new man to love, or at least to have an affair with.

Because of her obsession with Kane, she had never felt the slightest attraction to any other man. Yet, oddly enough, living so near Chris Donahue but free at last of her love for him, she had recently become strongly aware of her own body. It was quite a new experience, feeling a marked physical need without the blinding, delirious intoxication of being in love.

Her eyes wandered in the direction of the writer,

taking in the unconscious virility of his relaxed yet at the same time vibrantly alert body. She still didn't trust her new immunity to him and was therefore deeply relieved by his total lack of interest in her, but she was now determined to give other men a chance to awake in her the overwhelming pleasure she had known only with Kane.

A warm sensual wave washed through her, leaving her weak at the knees yet pleasantly excited about the future.

'Hey, Ariel, come back here.' Chris's dry voice cut through her thoughts. She felt her cheeks burning in a furious blush. 'You were miles away.'

Steeped in her thoughts, she hadn't noticed that Chris had left his place and was now standing very close to her, lazily leaning against her desk, his eyes scrutinising her flushed face with a mild interest.

'I was . . . I was just day-dreaming.' She stammered the non-committal answer.

'About your island, I bet.' He smiled down at her. 'Three years and still homesick, isn't that a bit much?'

'I'm not homesick.' She smiled back, having regained her composure. 'As a matter of fact, I was just giving myself a mental progress report.' She had learnt to answer his questions as candidly as she possibly could. Like Kane, he had that uncanny ability to detect the workings of her rich imagination.

Chris leaned back and stretched his arms lazily. 'So was I, as a matter of fact. And the long and the short of it is that I've had it. I'm beginning to feel like a fossil in this ghost-infested mausoleum of mine.'

'Thanks,' she said tartly.

'You're welcome, but I didn't mean to include you among the ghosts. You're delegated to the ranks of sprites and elves. Nifty little things, I rather think.'

'Not very reliable though,' she retorted in the same spirit. 'Have you finished going over the scene?'

'Yes, it's fine. We can start on the next one. Unless you'd rather stop for now.'

'Stop?' She looked at him stunned. 'It's not even five yet.'

'I know, but something tells me you're not too keen on working today.'

Once again, he had read her mind like an open book. 'Well, I wouldn't mind breaking for a stroll. It's such a nice day and . . .'

She stopped and stared at him, startled by the jarring sound of tyres on crunched gravel which announced the arrival of at least two cars. The sharp sound of slamming doors confirmed her suspicions that their jealously guarded isolation was being threatened to an invasion.

Chris groaned. 'Oh hell, are you expecting visitors?'

'Of course not,' she answered indignantly. 'I wouldn't dare even if I wanted to. What about you though? Have you invited anyone for the weekend?'

'You must be kidding.' He paused. 'Wait a minute. What's today?'

Neither had given much thought to the calendar over the last few days. She made a quick calculation in her head. 'The fourteenth!' she said and groaned.

'Daria's birthday party!' A rather off-colour word expressed Chris's feelings. 'Heaven knows what made me say they could use the house in the first place. I'd forgotten all about it. Marjorie did mutter something about it yesterday but knowing me, she should have reminded me again. Come to think of it,' he turned on Ariel, bristling with exasperation, 'so should you. You're supposed to be my secretary.'

'I'm not!' she sniped back. 'We both agreed to scrap that charade on my first night here. Besides,' she went on, frankly unrepentant, 'I couldn't be a secretary if my life depended on it. I'm hopeless when it comes to dates or appointments.'

'You pay for it, then, darling,' he said sweetly. 'We can forget about any more work for the rest of the weekend. I refuse to work in a house full of interfering so-and-sos. I'm off! The house and my relatives are all yours, and good luck to you too.'

'But . . . what do I say to them?'

'Anything you like . . . say I've got rabies. No, that probably won't deter those bitchy relatives of mine.

Say I've had a recurrent attack of amnesia and I'm lost to the world.' He was already striding away in the direction of the garage.

'The usual perfect exit line.' A lazy, melodious voice, uncannily like Chris's, came from behind her, making her whirl around with a startled gasp.

A tall, handsome man was standing by the study door, his amused grin unashamedly admitting that he had been eavesdropping on the last exchange between her and Chris.

'I wouldn't waste my breath trying to find an excuse for Chris's manners. We're all used to them by now,' he went on, chatting casually at her as he stepped into the room. 'My wife and Cynthia will be furious of course. But we are all used to that as well, so don't give it another thought. Just leave it all to me.'

She noted a marked resemblance to Chris in his colouring and height, but where her employer was given to handsome ruggedness and unyielding strength, this man obviously scored on boyish charm and good looks which were already going to seed.

'Miss Stewart, I presume?' He took her limp hand in his and shook it a little too warmly as his eyes ran up and down the length of her body with open but inoffensive appreciation. 'May I call you Ariel? I'm Neville Donahue, Chris's cousin. Older in years, but younger, oh, much younger in spirit.' She hardly needed the introduction. This was the man who stood in for Chris as general director of Donahue Enterprises. The one Paul Andrews accused of stepping far too eagerly into his cousin's shoes and refusing to let go when the missing man came back.

He was still holding on to her hand, ignoring her polite attempts to pull it away. 'We spoke on the phone several times. But knowing my cousin's temper, I never dared engage you in a lengthy conversation for fear of your life. Come on and join us for a drink.'

'Oh, I couldn't, Mr Donahue. I still have hours of typing to do and——' She tried to free herself from his persistent pull.

'Nonsense. As Chris has been selfish enough to

leave you alone and unprotected at the mercy of his predatory relatives, I see no reason why you should spend the weekend slaving away for him.' She was trying to decide whether his wry mocking tone was openly resentful or was just a self-conscious attempt to cover up the admiration with which he obviously regarded his cousin. 'And incidentally, would you mind very much calling me by my first name? Since I have the honour of sharing the title of "Mr Donahue" with my illustrious cousin, I'd rather not be addressed by it. It always makes me uncomfortably aware of his presence. My name is Neville, in case you didn't catch it.'

Ariel burst out laughing. 'Are you sure Daria is not your *real* daughter?'

'You mean, we both talk too much? Well, yes I suppose we do. Still, someone has to in our family. Chris certainly does less than his share, wouldn't you agree? Now, come in and meet the family. You'll have to sooner or later, so you might as well get it over with now.'

With the Donahues' typical disregard for other people's wishes, he gently but firmly propelled her into the adjoining lounge.

She had expected a whole crowd of people, but in fact, there were only three. Daria, looking uncharacteristically demure, was smiling up at her from a low ottoman, but Ariel's eyes were immediately drawn to Cynthia, lolling full length on one of the deep loungers at the other end of the vast room, looking stunning, as usual. The third woman, small and sharp-edged like a scrawny bird, had to be Grace, Daria's mother, with whom Ariel had had several exasperating telephone conversations over the last two weeks, all of which were obsessively concerned with details of Daria's party.

She was beautifully and expensively dressed and had obviously spent a long time on her make-up, but she still looked pathetically insecure and far older than her youthful husband. She was standing by the uncurtained glass wall, seemingly impervious to her surroundings, her eyes fixed on the gravelled path to the villa's front gates, refusing to acknowledge Ariel's existence. From her stiff disapproving bearing it was quite obvious that she had seen Chris drive away, and was still smarting at his refusal to show the slightest rudimentary regard for his guests.

Neville made straight to the drinks tray. 'Chris is gone,' he announced cheerfully to the world at large. 'An important last minute conference in . . . Timbuktu, I think he said. But I found something far better in the study. His temporary representative. So say hello nicely to her.'

His cheerful chatter brought a twinge of irritation to Grace's face, though her eyes remained fixed to the window. But Cynthia, teased to attention by a male voice, raised herself languidly on one elbow. 'I'll have another Kir, Neville,' she ordered languidly.

He obeyed the order good naturedly. 'I believe you've met Chris's Girl Friday, Cynthia, haven't you?'

Ariel winced at the trite title and waited patiently while Cynthia's beautiful green eyes made a deliberately slow journey up her shapeless boiler suit, pausing to inspect her short ruffled hair and her unpainted face before she smiled languidly and nodded in acknowledgment.

'Cynthia's another cousin. Twice removed, in Chris's case, so there's no risk of incest, in case you were wondering,' Neville explained patiently. 'We all grew up together, didn't we, pet? All except Grace, that is.' He threw his silent wife a hostile glance. 'She had joined the clan later. Oh, much, much later. When was it, my darling?' The over-sweet interest sounded almost sinister. 'Three—no, I lie, four years ago.'

It was Daria, looking ill at ease and angry, who put her stepfather in his place. 'You didn't offer Ariel a drink, Neville.'

Her rebuke had an instant effect. Neville's handsome face lost its sarcastic sneer, to be replaced by a sheepish grin. 'Sorry, love. I tend to forget my manners in my old home. I guess I revert to adolescence.'

'You don't need to revert, darling.' Cynthia's throaty laugh filled the room. 'You've never outgrown it. That's your charm, though, so don't you ever ever change, there's a love.'

The subtle, vicious bitching went way above Ariel's head. She had no idea what the hell they were talking about, which seemed to be part of their fun. The room was practically sizzling with thinly varnished loathing which was making her head spin.

'So how's the work going?' Cynthia now turned her large, green gaze on Ariel. She carefully chose her next dig so that there would be no doubt that she wasn't referring to the novel adaptation. 'When will Chris be finished with you, do you think?'

'I can't really tell yet——' Ariel began to explain and stopped to move aside as Neville settled next to her, his arm immediately finding a resting position behind her head, far too close for comfort.

'Well?' Cynthia held tenaciously to anything she sank her teeth in, her initial question in this case. 'What's your timetable? Another week? Two?'

Ariel put her half-empty glass on the low coffee-table, an immense eight-by-five-foot platform of beautifully weathered light oak. 'Who knows? The adaptation may take months.' She stressed the word 'adaptation', to counter Cynthia's bitchy allusions.

Grace, who had remained icily aloof, came to life, as if suddenly aware of Ariel's presence. 'Aren't you through working for today?'

'Not really, Mrs Donahue,' Ariel answered shortly. 'I still have quite a lot to do. Tomorrow as well.'

'Nonsense. You can't go on working throughout the weekend. I was actually counting on your bedroom being free. We're expecting quite a few people from out of town, you see. So why don't you tidy up and go home and have a nice rest till Monday?'

Neville Donahue was watching his nervous wife with undisguised amusement. 'I don't think she wants a nice rest, Grace.'

Ariel had had enough. 'I'm sorry, but Chris insisted I stay, Mrs Donahue, so much as I'd love to follow your advice, I can't go home. Now, if you'll all excuse me . . . I'm very behind in my work.' She tried to move but Neville's arm came down, keeping her prisoner in her seat.

Grace seemed to be torn between frustrated anger and a growing unease. 'But I . . . I'm afraid I didn't include you in the dinner list tomorrow,' she said half apologetically, half defiant.

'You see,' Cynthia joined in, sweetly, 'it's only for family and close friends.'

Ariel shrugged out of Neville's encircling arm and stood up. She wasn't going to take any more of this. 'Oh, that's quite all right, Mrs Donahue.' She was addressing Grace but her eyes were directed at Cynthia. 'As a matter of fact, Chris and I were planning to eat out tomorrow night. I've just booked a table at the Mayfair.' The lie was out before she could stop herself. She always fell into the same trap when finding herself in a tight corner or when her patience was sorely tried.

'You mean . . . he won't be here!' The strident whisper came from Grace. Cynthia's outrage erupted at the same time. 'How dare he! How dare he insult me like that!'

She didn't expect such a stormy reaction and she regretted that senseless stupid lie bitterly. All she needed now was for Chris to think that she had deliberately trapped him into an intimate dinner with her. She could protest till the cows came home that she had no intention of going out with him, he wouldn't believe her.

The strained silence was broken as Cynthia stood up and stormed out of the room, slamming the heavy oak door behind her.

Neville turned to her, looking genuinely contrite. 'Sorry about that, my dear. I'm afraid Cynthia gets a bit stroppy when things don't go exactly according to her plans.'

'If you'll excuse me, Mr Donahue,' she said coolly, trying to push past Chris's cousin, 'I really must go now. But I'll try to keep out of the study, if that would suit you better, Mrs Donahue. I can work in my room.'

Nobody tried to stop her as she walked out.

She had no intention of going back to work now. Smarting with resentment at Chris for leaving her alone with his horrid relatives, she stepped out of the house, determined to keep out of their way for as long as possible. Determinedly, she made straight to her Renault which had been parked for the last ten days in Chris's spacious garage. She hadn't used it once in all that time. It occurred to her that she might enjoy a leisurely wander and a bit of shopping in Hampstead village, perhaps even treat herself to a delicious continental coffee and cake at Louis's Patisserie. In fact, this was going to be her first foray into the outside world since she had started working with Chris.

She was slightly put off when she reached the garage. Daria, uncannily, must have guessed her next step and was already there, waiting for her. 'I knew it,' the girl greeted her unhappily. 'You're running away, aren't you?'

'Don't be silly,' Ariel said shortly. 'Why should I run away?'

'That's just it,' the young girl said, dejectedly. 'You shouldn't, not on account of my mother and Cynthia, anyway. I'm really sorry about them, Ariel. But now you see why Chris dislikes us all so much. I really don't know how to apologise for their behaviour. You mustn't mind Neville, though. He's a nice man, really, and he does love Chris. But he's so weak it's almost pathetic. And Cynthia . . .'

'Yes, what about Cynthia?' In spite of herself, she couldn't restrain her seething resentment for the sultry beauty.

'Well, she's jealous of you, of course.' Daria seemed bemused by her slow understanding. 'She resents Chris's spending all his time with you. He hasn't taken her out once since you started working together. She considers Chris her property, you see.'

'Her property? You mean, they're engaged?' Ariel broke in, shaken.

'Oh, not any more,' the girl assured her. 'Chris broke it off when he came back from his . . . from his trip. She has been married and divorced since but she is still convinced that they were meant for each other. She never gives up, our Cynthia.'

Daria was happily divulging every known detail concerning Cynthia's relationship with Chris, her failed marriage and her modelling career. But Ariel had stopped listening. Her mind was churning with the dawning understanding of something which had been nagging at her for years: Kane's fiercest reasons for objecting to marrying her had been a vague but very persistent feeling that he wasn't a free man. It now became clear to her that somewhere in the depths of his dark memory, he had retained an image of that beautiful, sophisticated woman whom he had known almost since childhood, and to whom he had committed himself.

'. . . and please don't feel too badly about my mother being so beastly to you. She was a little upset, I'm afraid . . .' Daria was still talking on, typically unaware of Ariel's absorption in her own thoughts. 'You see, she has always hoped that Chris would marry me one day. But now, since you have arrived on the scene . . .'

'What?' Daria's casual words suddenly caught Ariel's attention. 'What exactly do you mean by that, Daria? You don't think that Chris and I . . .'

The girl smiled at Ariel's shocked expression. 'I don't mean anything,' she said quietly. 'But just for the record, I want you to know that I'm no rival, no more than Cynthia is. I might have had a chance once, but I lost it the moment he heard you laugh.' A cunning little smile transformed for a moment the usually guileless freckled face, warning Ariel that any further denials and protestations would be quite useless.

The two girls stared silently at each other for a long moment. And then Daria giggled, the carefree, innocent mask back on. 'Aren't you lucky to be out with Chris tomorrow night? At least you'll be spared another nasty scene from the Donahues' domestic repertoire. I'm sorry you won't be at my party though. I really do like you, you see.'

Ariel smiled at her. 'It's mutual,' she said sincerely.

'Oh, I know. I'm irresistible,' she giggled and was gone.

Shaken as she was by Daria's latest revelations, Ariel couldn't help giggling to herself, as she reversed out of the garage. She was crawling past the villa's gate and along the quiet alley engrossed in her thoughts, when her stomach leapt to her throat. A flash went past her with a deafening roar, making her skid off the road at the last minute. She switched off the engine and sat for a second, trying to calm the pounding of her heart.

'Where exactly were you thinking of going?' The lazy, low voice revived her numbed senses like a sharp slap.

'You're mad, Chris!' She attacked him when she found her voice. 'Surely there are easier ways of getting rid of an unwanted collaborator than murder by heart attack.' Only now she saw the silver Porsche, parked a few yards away, in front of her car.

Chris wasn't smiling as he wrenched open the door of her Renault. 'Sorry, I did honk several times but nothing seemed to shake you out of your day-dream. So, where are you off to?'

'To Hampstead, for a few hours away from work and . . .'

'Away from me,' he finished for her, perceptive as usual.

'If you say so,' she agreed crossly. 'I see no reason why I should be the one to deal with your squabbling relatives while you feel free to zoom off.'

Chris responded with a wry chuckle which a few days ago would have evoked the painful memory of Kane, but now was as much part of the real man as the amused glint in his deep blue eyes and the twist of his firm, generous mouth. 'Well, the same idea has occurred to me. I was actually coming back to get you out of there when I saw you crawling by. You've been day-dreaming again, have you?'

'No,' she said shortly. 'As a matter of fact, I was thinking of your family. Daria, among others . . .' she admitted candidly.

'And?'

'Cynthia,' she admitted sulkily, cursing his shrewd reading of her mind.

'Ah, the lovely golden-haired Cynthia ... the long lost love of my youth. How did you like her?' He didn't wait for her reply. 'Don't answer that. I can now see why you ran screaming to your car. Do you think a short jog around the Heath could calm you down?'

She hesitated. There was nothing unusual about their jogging together. They had been in the habit of doing so regularly every evening, to stretch their muscles after hours of work. But this was different. They weren't working now and something about the way he had suggested it made it sound almost as if he was asking her out. Squirming uneasily, she suddenly remembered the silly lie she had told the family about them going out to dinner together the next day.

'Well?' he pursued, already wrenching open the door on her side.

'I was rather looking forward to a walk around the village. I need to do some shopping and . . .'

'You can have Monday morning off for that. Come on, Ariel. Just a short jog up to that clump of trees over there. I promise I won't make you do the usual mileage.'

Laughing, she allowed him to pull her out of the car, and obeying an odd need to keep a distance between them, broke into a fast jog down the deserted alley leading to the Heath. He overtook her within a few seconds and with hardly a look at her, he went on jogging easily up the slope, leaving her behind.

He was waiting for her, leaning against the thick bark of a huge elm tree, looking fresh and relaxed as if he had just got out of bed, when she finally reached it.

Panting, she flopped down on the cool grass, throwing herself backwards, her eyes shut, trying to calm her tortured lungs.

'Feeling better?' Chris's lazy drawl came floating down from above her after a few minutes.

She nodded, refusing to open her eyes.

'You ought to go back home,' he said. She could sense his measured gaze studying her spent body. 'This country is turning your muscles into cotton wool.'

Something in that infuriatingly unexerted voice made her taunt him back, unwise as she knew it was. 'What makes you think I was any better back home?'

'You told me,' he said and suddenly stopped and turned to her, the hint of suspicion in his voice. 'Or did you?'

'I guess I did. I talk so much I hardly remember what I say.' She sat up, suddenly feeling too exposed to his piercing gaze, lying flat on her back as she was.

The Heath was utterly deserted now, slowly enwrapped by the lengthening shadows of twilight and the thick belt of elm trees was an isolating cocoon, shutting off the sight of the few mansions which dotted the fringes of the park. Lulled by the tranquillity around them, they drifted into a comfortable, unstrained silence, listening to the steady, distant murmur of the city traffic. Curiously it brought to mind the sound of the ocean.

As always their thoughts seemed to follow the same drift. 'I've kept away from my yacht far too long,' he said softly. 'I miss my sea-legs.'

'I'd rather have my feet safe on land,' she responded with a chuckle. 'I like sailing but I prefer to return to my rock-steady home at the end of the day.'

'You would, of course. Still, could you bear to spend several weeks at sea?' The question came out so casually that it never occurred to her it had any meaning beyond a mild, conversational interest.

'I guess I could, but not on my own. I can bear my own company only so much, you know.'

'And with me?'

Ariel laughed, a little breathlessly, adept by now at hiding how his unintentionally cruel teasing twisted her insides. 'Oh, with you, that's an entirely different proposition.'

'We could even make a short visit to your island,' he went on, calmly. 'My yacht, as it happens, is moored

in the Seychelles. Another one of those coincidences,'
he finished drily.

There it was again, that ugly mocking hint at his
being wise to her. Let him, she bristled silently. She
was tired of avoiding those pitfalls. Defiantly, she took
up the bait. 'I wonder what made you switch to the
Indian Ocean? I read in some old press clips that your
cruising ground used to be the Caribbean.'

'That's as may be, but the Indian Ocean happens to be
my favourite *hunting* ground.'

'Hunting?' she repeated, puzzled. 'Hunting what?'

'My mislaid memory, darling. That's where I lost
it.'

She was taken aback. It was the first time he'd
answered her direct question without a wry set-down
for stepping beyond the agreed boundaries. 'In the
Seychelles islands?' she asked carefully.

There was a sparkling glint in his eyes as he turned
them on her. 'Either there or on some other island in
the Indian Ocean. I don't know for sure. I can only
tell you that I found it again in Mahe. In hospital, to
be more precise. Apparently, I'd collapsed just outside
Victoria airport, they told me. Passed out, without any
apparent reason. They had no idea who I was or how I
got there. I wasn't much help either. The last thing I
remembered was flying over the Indian Ocean in my
small jet with one wing on fire, telling myself, in the
immortal words of Peter Pan, that "dying could be
such a big adventure".'

'You did know who you were, though?'

He frowned, as if he found her question rather dim.

'Of course I knew who I was. But for the life of me
I couldn't account for my being in Mahe nearly six
months after my plane crashed, without papers, credit
cards or any other means of identification. The only
connection I had with my dark past was a rather
attractive beard which I reluctantly shaved off when I
got back home.'

'I suppose a beard would look rather good on you,'
she was amazed to hear herself say.

'Well, I could grow it again, if you asked nicely.'

'I might at that, if it could get you to work half an hour earlier every morning so that you wouldn't keep me working till midnight. And speaking of time,' she added, disturbed by the dangerous note of intimacy which seemed to have crept in, the suggestive note in the lazy voice, 'don't you think we ought to be getting back?'

She began to struggle to her feet.

'Wait, Ariel.' His hand detained her. 'I meant what I said, you know. If we keep getting along as well as we have done so far, we may as well do the bulk of the adaptation aboard my yacht. We'd be far better off without all those phone calls and the imminent threat of my family's sudden descent on us.'

She couldn't help feeling a warm glow of satisfaction. 'Does that mean I'm no longer on trial?' She kept her voice studiously cool.

Chris gave her an impassive look. 'You've known it since your first night in the house. So don't play coy with me, Ariel.'

'Sorry,' she admitted readily. 'I just wasn't sure.'

'Right,' he announced and struggled to his feet, pulling her up after him. 'So now that you know, would you consider moving the office to my yacht?'

Ariel took a deep breath. She was playing with fire but it was too late to back off now. 'Certainly. When do we go?'

There was a momentary pause, which he finally ended. 'Not for a few days. I feel I ought to give you time to think it over, before you decide.'

She smiled. 'You mean, before *you* decide, don't you? For myself, I'd like that very much. But I guess you'll need to be convinced beyond any shadow of doubt that I won't be impinging on your privacy. So, by all means, let's wait.'

Instead of responding to her with a chuckle, Chris shook his head.

'That's not exactly it, Ariel.' He spoke softly. 'I have to be sure that I won't be impinging on yours.'

'It's quite all right. I'm not as jealous about my privacy as you are,' she laughed.

'Perhaps not,' he said easily. 'But you do realise that you'll be sharing more than just working hours with me.'

'But I wouldn't mind. In fact, I quite like being with you,' she said unguardedly, still perplexed by his odd insistence.

'Like this too?' he asked in the same casual tone, and foolishly she turned around to ask, 'Like what?'

His head swooped down on hers without any warning, stunning her into a momentary surprise. And before she could react, her shoulders were caught by two strong hands, robbing her of her chance to escape his kiss.

She stiffened but wasn't particularly alarmed, anticipating the same contemptuous, unfeeling embrace of the first night which had left her cold and unmoved. But in an instant she knew that this time he wasn't acting out of anger or disdain as he had done then. There was no fire or hunger in his lips as they covered her mouth, coolly attempting to coax her participation with airy, calculating kisses. He seemed to be sussing her out, as if he was conducting a mildly intriguing experiment.

Her first instinct was to resist him. This is not Kane, she warned herself frantically. Don't let him do this to you. You mean nothing to him! But even as she struggled to pull away from his firm, persistent lips, she felt the old familiar ache in the pit of her stomach and the tingle of excitement which ran like an electric current throughout her body, and she shut her mind to the warning bell.

She had been asking for this for days, allowing herself to feel attracted to him, daring her body to wallow in memories of the heady pleasures she had been repressing for so long. So why fight it now?

She let her clenched fists unfold to rest flat against the rough texture of his sweat-shirt and her tightly compressed lips relaxed with a low moan and she could hear Chris's amused chuckle which seemed to congratulate her on her decision.

As if satisfied with the outcome of the experiment,

his hands left her shoulders to clasp her head between
them, and as her lips surrendered under the pressure of
his mouth, she felt the thrilling invasion of his tongue
and she sagged against his hard chest, raising her arms to
clasp his back, hungry to feel his body again.

But instead of his taking advantage of her willing
surrender, she suddenly was aware of a curious,
disturbing stillness in him.

He raised his head. 'Ariel?' His low voice was
questioning, uncertain.

She knew even before she opened her eyes that he
was no longer the confident, thrilling stranger who
was just amusing himself with her aroused senses. The
cloudy blue gaze which met hers was scouring her face
with the old agonising bewilderment which she
remembered so well.

A wave of heart-wrenching love gripped her and she
pulled his head down, her lips opening in a mute
attempt to drown his agony in her kiss, and with an
old sense of triumph she felt the shudder go through
his tense body as he gathered her into his arms in an
impatient, crushing embrace.

There was nothing of the calculating, teasing
seducer as he pushed her down against the dewy grass,
his mouth reclaiming hers with a savage, unconscious
hunger for something which had been denied him for
so long. The upper part of his body was crushing her
down with the harshness of his ungoverned need, his
hands struggling to rediscover the familiar curves of
her hips, her thighs, her breasts, under the thick layer
of her clothing.

The alarm bell was ringing furiously in her mind
but she refused to stop now. She was too far gone
now, pulsating with the rediscovery of his demanding
body and her own reawakened hunger to care or think
about the consequences. She was responding to his
harsh, angry exploration with her old uninhibited
abandon, her hands pushing underneath his clothes to
savour the smooth surface of his hard naked flesh,
loving the feel of his muscles as they contracted and
quivered with the delight of her touch.

But as she began to sink into a well of wild, mindless sensuality, her body already striving towards the inevitable culmination of its escalating hunger, she was vaguely, uneasily aware of his long, sensitive fingers pushing through her hair, searching blindly, almost frantically for the long tresses which were no longer there. And she knew, even before she felt his body freeze into immobility, that the fragile link which he had just made with his dead memory had been severed by the unfamiliar texture of her short, cropped hair and she could no longer imagine herself back in the past. All at once, she became miserably aware of the wet hard ground underneath her and the heavy weight of his body on top of hers.

'Jesus, Ariel!' He gave a shaken laugh as he pushed his head back so that he could see her face. 'I didn't realise I wanted you that badly.'

The voice was Chris Donahue's, wry, self-mocking, in control again. Yet something in his tone tore through her embarrassed shame, making her forget her own vulnerability and reach out to him, aching with understanding of his sudden awareness of a hunger he had been unconscious of until this very minute. But as he lowered his head again, ready to continue where they had just left off, she became all too aware of the hopeless muddle into which she had allowed herself to be swept.

With a thrusting push, she freed herself of his unguarded hold and rolled away, to lie alone, her lungs drinking the air in short gasps which mingled with Chris's tortured breathing.

A soft rustle by her side told her that he had sat up, and conscious of her half-naked body, she clumsily pulled her sweat-shirt over her exposed breasts. It was dark now, under the canopy of the elms, and Chris was just a looming shadow a few feet away from her, carefully adhering to the distance that she had created between them.

'You're right, of course.' He was still struggling to catch his breath, his voice husky with the raw vulnerability of his aroused desire. 'We'd better stop now and go back home. We'll be far more comfortable in my room.'

'What . . . what do you mean?' she asked, her voice tight.

He waited for his breathing to steady down a little before he answered. 'I mean that my earlier suggestion of waiting till we board my yacht doesn't apply any more. To put it bluntly, Ariel, there's no way I could keep my hands off you for that long and my bedroom seems the most sensible solution right now. Unless you have a better idea.'

She listened to him, appalled by his arrogant assumption of their becoming lovers and at the same time rigid with shame, remembering the total abandon with which she had responded to his lovemaking. 'I . . . I'd rather you forgot what has just happened,' she mumbled, her voice tight with embarrassment. 'I didn't mean to go so far. I'm sorry.'

He wasn't expecting that, she could tell by the long silence which followed her stammering rejection.

'I see,' he said finally. 'I suppose the rest of you is kept in cold storage for the mysterious Kane, when or if he ever deigns to come back. Is that it?'

'K . . . Kane?' she stammered, not sure she had heard him properly.

'The once and future Kane,' he misquoted, reading her shocked response as an embarrassed admission of her foolish, adolescent loyalty. 'The man who's gone away.'

In a shock, it suddenly dawned on her that not once during that passionate eruption did she imagine herself in the arms of Kane. The ghost had finally been exorcised from her heart. It was Chris Donahue who broke through her defences. And it was Chris Donahue, not Kane, she wanted to give herself to. And not just her body either. Whether he wanted it or not, Chris had inherited all the stubborn, unreasonable love she had for Kane.

'Oh, well.' She heard him chuckling softly to himself. 'So much for my male chauvinist smugness. I could have sworn you were just as eager as me to carry on till the sweet end.'

'I'm sorry,' she whispered miserably.

'Don't feel too bad about it, love. I only hope Kane is capable of appreciating such loyalty. You know,' he went on, in sincere, unresentful puzzlement, 'I never doubted for a moment that you were mine for the asking. It just didn't feel right to take advantage of your willing body just to satisfy what seemed to me like a mild case of attraction on my part. Mild!' He gave a short bark of a laugh. 'Damn it, Ariel, I could eat you alive, flesh, blood and delicious bones right here and now! And to hell with my scruples, or more to the point, to hell with that elusive Kane of yours.'

A tight, unnatural giggle escaped her lips as a wave of hysteria was threatening to take hold of her stunned mind. She buried her head in her hands, not sure whether her quivering lips were about to break out in sobs or in a fit of giggles.

Gently he pushed her hands away and placed a fist under her chin to force her to look at him. 'Come on, Ariel,' he went on. 'Don't you think it's time you gave up on that prodigal heart-throb?'

'It's nothing to do with Kane,' she tried to explain. 'And it's nothing to do with me either. It's not me you want, but some phantom which you have buried in your memory.'

He didn't try to deny it. 'All right, then,' he said softly. 'I'll make a deal with you, Ariel. Since we both seem to be haunted by phantoms, let's help each other get them out of our system. I'm quite willing to use you as a substitute and quite frankly, darling, I don't think it would be too difficult to exorcise the spirit of Kane out of your very willing and lovely body. How about it?'

A groan escaped her stiff lips and she shook her head mutely. She couldn't take any more of his unintentionally cruel taunting.

'Well, Ariel? It's up to you now.' He prompted, as his hand once again reached for her head, no longer bewildered by the short cropped hair. 'Where do we go from here?' Certain of his power over her now, he pulled her towards him, about to sign off the argument with another convincing kiss.

Angrily she pulled away from his tightening grip. 'We go nowhere,' she said tightly. 'Unless it's to continue working together as we have done until now.'

His sparkling eyes were smiling down on her with easy, friendly mockery. 'Oh, we'll go on working, no fear of that. But don't delude yourself that we're going to stop where we started a few minutes ago. You're in for a full-scale seduction campaign. And what's more, you'd better take your capitulation for granted.'

'You arrogant bas——' she started to spit back at his insufferable grinning face.

'Well, yes, I suppose I am,' he agreed easily, amused by her anger. 'You see, I haven't lost a battle yet . . . those I took the trouble to fight, I mean.'

'Oh God! Can't you understand?' She tried to break through to him. 'I don't want to——'

He ignored her feeble attempts to explain herself. In one easy move, he was on his feet, pulling her up after him. 'Oh yes, you do. It's too late to back off now, Ariel. I didn't seek you out, remember? You came after me. Well, you've got what you wanted. What we both want,' he conceded drily.

'You're wrong, so wrong.' She tried to stand up, desperate to get away from him now. 'What you want and what I want are two different things.'

His strong hand held her down. 'No, they're not. We both want to bury the ghosts. Or at least, find a satisfactory substitute, so that you can say goodbye to that Kane of yours, and I can give up a hopeless dream of ever finding some faceless phantom.'

His face was hovering above her, hardly an inch away, and suddenly she was tired of fighting herself. It was pointless, anyway, and she wanted him so badly, she ached. She felt the pull of his hand and sagged against him, shutting her eyes in a silent submission to the inevitable kiss, but instead he just pushed her off, stood up and pulled her to her feet.

'Not here, Ariel,' he said drily. 'We can continue

this conversation in my bedroom. Come on, I'll race you back to the house.' He started running easily down the gentle slope in the direction of the glinting lights of the villa, not waiting to see whether she was following him.

She made her way down slowly, making no attempt to keep up with him. She needed to be alone to pull herself together, make some sense of what had just happened. It seemed incredible that only two hours ago she had been sitting calmly in the study, congratulating herself on her recovery from her obsession with the past and looking forward to a new free future. The irony was that she indeed had been cured of her old problem, but only to be trapped, more hopelessly than ever, in a new muddle.

She had no idea how she was going to repulse Chris's next confident assault on her tottering will-power but there was no doubt in her mind that the last hour on the Heath marked the beginning of a long, disastrous chute from which she would probably never recover. And she had no one to blame but herself.

She had totally forgotten about the invading Donahues until she was inside the villa's gates and saw the offending cars parked on the gravelled area at the front of the villa.

Chris was waiting for her by the front door, washed in the bright lights which poured out of the lounge's wide windows. Grace was still standing in the same spot, as if she had never left her guard behind the uncurtained glass, her face set in a grim, unhappy mask as she watched Ariel making her slow reluctant way to Chris's side. Between Chris's determination to drag her to his bed and his hostile family already suspecting some such intention, Ariel was beginning to feel utterly trapped.

'We've forgotten the family yet again, love, haven't we?' he said the moment she reached him, smiling down at her. 'It doesn't really matter, though. Just bring your car back here and leave it in the garage. One of my men will drive it back to Dulwich on Monday morning. And don't bother packing up all your things. Just take enough to get you going for the next few days. We can buy whatever you need when we get there.'

'Get where? Buy what? I don't know what you're talking about, Chris,' she grumbled, utterly bewildered now.

'We're going to stay in a small country hotel until we leave for the Seychelles,' he explained patiently. 'I'll get the office to book us on the first available flight.'

She stamped her foot in helpless fury. 'Will you please listen to me, Chris! I'm not going anywhere with you.'

'Oh yes you are, my darling,' he informed her calmly. 'We've unfinished business to attend to. And I'm not talking about that blasted adaptation either.'

She turned away from him, about to stamp off, but his hand came down to grab her shoulder and pull her back straight into his arms, in full view of the watchful Grace behind the glazed window.

'Let me go,' she hissed. 'They are watching!'

'Good for them,' he said in his most infuriating arrogance. 'And let's not have any more futile arguments, Ariel. I don't know why you're fighting me like this. You're certainly not the type to be acting coy. But whatever your reason, let's just end it here and now. You want me, I want you, and that's that.'

Smiling at her furious expression, he tightened his arms around her and before she could avert her face, took her breath with a long, hard kiss which left her weak at the knees.

'You see what I mean?' he said lightly, amusedly aware of her shaken reaction. 'Now go and pack. I'll just get the manuscript and a few things together and meet you here in ten minutes.' And with a slight undignified smack he pushed her in the direction of the main door while he walked off in the direction of the study patio.

She remained standing where she was for a few undecided moments. When she looked up, she met Neville's eyes, grinning at her broadly from behind the glass. Grace was no longer standing by the window but Ariel had no doubt that the whole family had been enjoying a very good view of Chris's performance. She knew instantly that there was only one thing for her to do now. Briskly, she turned her back on the house and hurriedly covered the few hundred yards up the lane towards the main road, where she had left her Renault hardly an hour ago. It seemed like a whole lifetime now. By the time Chris emerged from the house, ready to take off, her small black car had already become just one more unremarkable item in the endless, uniform line of evening traffic which threaded its way towards the centre of town.

CHAPTER EIGHT

THE large Victorian Dulwich house felt gloomier than ever after those few days in Chris Donahue's villa. Michael was out and hadn't left a note since he hadn't been expecting her, but she assumed that he was out with Lindsay, a second-year intern in the same hospital, who had been his regular girl-friend for almost a year now.

Ariel braced herself for a fight, then picked up the phone and dialled Paul's number. When he answered, she told him she was quitting. 'I'm no good for him, Paul. I've never done a film before, only television one-offs and episodes in series. He would be far better off with a proper script-writer.'

'You tell *him* that,' Paul spat out disgustedly. 'And you're talking nonsense. He isn't complaining, is he? In fact, I believe he's very pleased with you. For God's sake, girl,' his voice rose in exploding anger, 'after days of teasing and taunting, he calls me up and tells me that he's not only decided to keep you on but has agreed to sign the contract with Garland. And now you come and tell me you don't want to do it!'

'I'm sorry,' she mumbled weakly.

'Well, you can't back out now. And that's final. What the hell's come over you anyway? Only two weeks ago you were ready to trade ten years of your life for the chance of working with him.'

She was silent.

'Listen, Ariel. I refuse to do anything unless you give me a good reason. You're behaving like a spoilt, half-witted child. Why can't you go on working with him, now that he actually wants you to?'

'I just can't. Please, Paul. You've got to help me. I just can't go on. Not any more.'

Finally the old agent gave in. 'God knows where I'll find a replacement, though,' he ended, wearily. 'Chris has already vetoed the best people I had.'

'He'll be less difficult now, Paul,' Ariel promised him. 'He's really cottoned on to the technical side and he won't feel cramped by the professionals. In fact, he could actually carry on alone now, if you ask me.'

'Oh yes? Can you see him typing?'

Ariel's smile hid her pain. Kane had become an ace typist and, like riding a bicycle, it was a skill once learnt never lost. 'I certainly can,' she said calmly. 'I shouldn't worry about that, Paul. Just call him tomorrow and tell him I won't be coming back on Monday. I'll have someone go over and collect my things later this week.'

She replaced the receiver and for a good hour, wandered around the house, inventing unnecessary chores to keep herself busy, perversely ranting at Michael's tidy habits which hardly left her any work. To her annoyance, she found herself comparing her brother with Chris, chuckling ruefully at the latter's total disregard for order. If Chris were left on his own, without her or Marjorie to tidy up after him, the house would be a complete shambles after a few hours.

Stop thinking about him, she ordered herself, flinging a redundant duster disgustedly back into the drawer.

Her room offered no comfort, but at least here she found something with which to occupy herself. She wasn't a messy person by nature, only a compulsive paper-hoarder who couldn't bear to throw away even the least significant note. The wall-shelves, desk-drawers, even the floor, were piled high with discarded drafts, numerous versions of earlier scripts, files of personal and professional letters and notes. It was the proud accumulation of three years of a successful career but it was crying out for a thorough clear-up. With a forced burst of energy she threw herself into the arduous task, as if by tidying up the cluttered debris of the last years, she was also clearing up the illusions and false hopes which had been cluttering her mind ever since Kane had left her.

She was even beginning to find some pleasure in the tangible results of her efforts, but as if the whole world conspired against her, she found herself clutching a piece of paper, flimsy and grey with age, which she had carried away with her when she left St Patrick. It was Kane's first and last love-letter which she had found after his departure:

'Just remember whenever you think of me: no matter how treacherous my memory has been in the past, it'll always remain faithful to you.' She re-read the words she already knew by heart. 'My heart tells me that I have never loved anyone as I love you and my whole being shouts out that I shall never love anyone else. So, my love, till we meet again, Kane.'

Until now, the written words had always helped to renew her flagging hopes and strengthen her de-termination to find him again. But as she read them now she started to cry softly, at last giving in to the despair which had been lurking numb and heavy behind her forced activity. Kane's promise hammered in a final nail in the coffin of her love for Chris. He had kept his word, she thought, resigned. His buried memory did remain faithful to a nameless phantom from a lost island, and the fact that the ghost was none other than herself, the flesh-and-blood Ariel, made no difference. As far as Chris was concerned she was just another woman. And as Kane had written three years ago, he would never love another woman again.

The gloomy old house was echoing with eerie,

lonely silence. It wasn't nine o'clock yet, and the evening still stretched before her, vacant and lonely, full of despairing thoughts.

But the image of Chris Donahue kept barging in, sending shivers of aroused sensuality through her body, reviving the hour she had spent with him on the Heath. The comforting memory of Kane was pushed deeper and deeper into its grave.

Well, she had given both up now. She had bid Kane goodbye and walked out of the job with Chris at the same time. He wouldn't come after her, of that she was sure. He might have been aroused and disturbed by their lovemaking, but he still only thought of her as just another case of 'acute attraction', as opposed to the 'mild' case he had thought it was: a substitute for his lost 'phantom'. As long as she was around, he wasn't going to be deterred by her pathetically weak objections. But once she walked away, he was certainly not going to try and bring her back. He could easily get whatever he needed from someone like Cynthia. And if he still hankered after a substitute, there was always Daria to satisfy his subconscious memory of the island waif, if he ever came to regard her as a woman and not just a lovable nuisance.

As for herself, she couldn't settle for a substitute. She wanted him more than ever before. Her aroused senses were yearning for him with such an unremitting ache that she could barely stop herself from rushing back to him that very night. Yet she couldn't do it. No matter how badly she wanted Chris, she couldn't barter the unique, all-engulfing love she had once shared with Kane for a few weeks of loveless ecstasy.

She waited till long past midnight for Michael to come home. She needed to talk to him, tell him about Chris, and let his intelligent reasoning strengthen her own resolution. But finally she gave up expecting him home that night. He had been spending several nights a week in Lindsay's flat which was far more convenient to get to the West London hospital from in the morning. In fact, Ariel had been suspecting for some time now that the only reason Michael hadn't moved in with Lindsay was his reluctance to leave his sister alone in the large Dulwich house.

She went to bed, feeling even lonelier than before, thinking of how empty her life would be without Michael's constant and cheerful company. Maybe she should go back to St Patrick, she wondered as she drifted into sleep. It's true that her island was still alive with the presence of Kane, but now she would welcome those fading, sweet memories. At least they would be of some comfort against the trenchant agony of her rejected love for Chris.

She woke up to a house alive with sounds and people. When she stumbled, still half asleep, into the kitchen to investigate, she found Michael, still in his pyjamas, and Lindsay, wearing one of Michael's dressing-gowns, contentedly sipping their grapefruit juice. At the sight of her, Lindsay snatched her hand away from Michael's and both greeted her sheepishly, embarrassed and uncomfortable at being caught in such compromising circumstances.

Forgetting her own problems for a moment, Ariel fell into her characteristic bubbly, charming self, and finally managed to put Lindsay at her ease and relieve Michael of his own awkward guilt.

'I hope it wasn't me who stopped you from coming here before,' she said candidly to Lindsay, when she was sure the young woman was no longer smarting with embarrassment.

'Well, Michael felt that——' Lindsay faltered.

'That I'm a fragile little flower who mustn't be exposed to the facts of life, is that it?' Ariel filled in, looking laughingly at Michael. 'Or were you afraid I'd be jealous, seeing that I don't have a regular boy-friend myself?'

From his half-hearted chuckle she gathered that she had hit the nail on the head and her heart sank. She seemed to create obstacles wherever she went. Chris Donahue refused to open his heart to any woman because of a promise he had made to her in his phantom past and now her brother didn't dare bring his girl-friend home for fear of hurting her. Still, in

Michael's case, she had no trouble removing the obstacle. But there was no way she could release Chris from his self-inflicted banishment. If she told him the truth about Kane, he would feel bound to her by honour. And if she just left him, as she was about to do, he would still be imprisoned by that lost love.

She wasn't allowed to brood for long. They had hardly finished breakfast before Michael recruited both his girl-friend and his sister to help with the preparations for a Sunday lunch. He was a wonderful cook and loved demonstrating his skills. And today, like almost every Sunday, he had invited several friends and colleagues to sample his art.

It was long past seven when Ariel finally put the last dried glass in the china cabinet and went upstairs, leaving Michael in the lounge, happily wallowing in their favourite Mozart record which he put on at an ear-splitting volume, while Lindsay drove their guests home.

Soon, she abandoned her tired body to the refreshing tingle of a hot shower, her ears straining against the noise of the running water to catch Kiri Te Kanawa's lovely voice pouring out the Countess's unhappy love for her straying husband. It took a good few moments before she became aware of another sound: the doorbell was clamouring for attention with a shrill persistence which indicated that it had been ringing away for quite a while.

She waited a few seconds, expecting Michael to see to it, but he must have fallen asleep, or was still too sunk in his pleasant alcoholic stupor to hear anything. Finally, she grabbed a towel, quickly dabbed herself dry and wrapped a square piece of colourful cotton around her naked body, leaving her shoulders and arms bare. It was a sort of sarong which she used to wear regularly in St Patrick and still kept in London, as a substitute dressing-gown.

The persistent intruder must have given up, because the ringing had stopped abruptly before she reached the hall. Still, she went to the door and peered out into the chilly night, in case she could still catch whoever it was before he disappeared.

She was just in time. A tall, shadowy figure of a man was about to step into a car which looked suspiciously like a Porsche. But hearing the sound of the opening door, he turned back just in time to catch sight of her, the bright light behind her shining through her flimsy sarong.

Gripped by momentary panic, she stupidly tried to close the door but Chris was too quick for her. In his typical long, graceful strides, he gulped the few steps and reached the front door, his dark blue eyes daring her to shut the door in his face.

'Sorry,' she laughed, deeply embarrassed by her idiotic behaviour. 'I don't know why I did that. I guess you took me by surprise.'

'You acted quite rightly, you know.' Chris smiled down at her. 'Not many men could resist the temptation, seeing you in that thing you're wearing. May I come in?'

'Oh, of course. Do.' She hurriedly stepped back, her muscles tightening as he went past her, their bodies almost touching.

She shut the door against the cool night air, shivering slightly in her light wrap-up, and stood undecided in the hall, not knowing what to do next. 'Michael ... my brother's in the lounge, asleep, I'm afraid.'

'Asleep? With this racket going on?' The Mozart record was still going strong, with Cherubino's clear voice serenading the Countess. 'No wonder you didn't hear me ringing.'

Ariel shrugged. 'We had a huge lunch and we all got slightly drunk.' She giggled, suddenly feeling as awkward as a schoolgirl. 'I ... I don't know where to take you.'

'Not to your bedroom,' he suggested, gravely. 'I don't think it'd be wise, dressed as you are. That's a very welcome reminder of the Seychelles, by the way. Now I can actually picture you against the backdrop of luscious green foliage, white sand and deep blue water.

Odd, isn't it?' he went on, chatting casually. 'I never could before, you know. Shall we try the kitchen?'

She was too startled by his remark about the Seychelles to grasp the drift of his question. 'I beg your pardon?'

'Since your bedroom is out and the lounge is occupied, I could wait for you in the kitchen. With a cup of coffee, if it's not too much trouble.'

'Oh dear, I'm sorry. Of course.' She led him to the kitchen and he made straight to the kettle. 'I'll put the kettle on while you go upstairs and change,' he suggested.

'Change?'

'Well, this is an enchanting outfit, of course, and I'm sure you'll turn quite a few heads at the Mayfair but I hardly think it's the right thing for London at this time of year.'

She gaped at him for a second. 'I don't understand,' she said finally. 'What's the Mayfair got to do with it?'

'Isn't it where you and I are supposed to dine tonight?'

'We are?'

'Don't you remember? You and I had a date for tonight. At least, that's the impression you gave Cynthia yesterday.'

Ariel groaned. She had totally forgotten the silly white lie she had told the Donahues. 'Oh, come on, Chris. It was just a way to get you out of tonight's dinner party. I never meant you to actually take me out and you bloody well know it. So stop teasing me.'

'Sorry, love, but you're stuck. You robbed me of a delicious dinner, even if it did include my loving family, so now you pay up. I'm starving and it wasn't easy to organise a table at the Mayfair at such short notice. I had to promise the manager a tutorial session on his new computer to get it. So hurry up, darling, I'll take care of the coffee. Don't worry.'

With a gentle slap on her bottom, he sent her scurrying out of the kitchen and up the stairs, to her room.

She dressed in a daze, hardly knowing what she was

putting on, her head spinning with questions. He seemed quite affable, dangerously so if she knew Chris Donahue. There was no indication that Paul Andrews had already contacted him and told him about her decision to walk out on him. Yet, one never knew, either with Kane or with Chris Donahue. Both were champions at hiding their emotions behind that cool, laid-back, unflappable charm. He was obviously here to taunt her, but whether because of her decision to leave or her idiotic rash lie to Cynthia, she couldn't tell.

With an exasperated curse, she pulled off the shoes she had just put on: it was an unmatching pair. More alert now, she examined herself carefully in the mirror. This was, after all, the first time she had ever been taken out by either Kane or Chris, and in spite of herself, she wanted to look her best on her first ever date with either of them. She finally decided that the trendy natural linen Kenzo dress and the heavy leather belt which gathered its loose folds to her narrow waist wouldn't shame the most exclusive restaurant in London. The almost masculine cut made the most of the fragile femininity of her shape and she felt neither over-dressed nor conspicuously trendy in the dress's strong, clean lines, and the superb natural fabric. Her face looked pale and drawn in the harsh light of her bedroom but she decided against using make-up. She very rarely did and she had already spent more than fifteen minutes getting ready. The last thing she wanted was for Chris Donahue to think that she had taken special trouble to please him.

Suddenly furious at him for seeing everything in the most sardonic light and at herself for being so sensitive to his opinion, she perversely chose the large, tatty canvas bag she always wore for work and which clashed glaringly with the general cool elegance of her outfit, and rushed down the stairs, anticipating Chris's mocking remark at her expense but utterly unprepared for the disaster which awaited her.

She was halfway down the stairs when she saw Michael stagger out of the lounge, looking sleepy but very pleased with life. Only now she noticed that the house was no longer vibrating with the sounds of the opera. The silence was almost eerie now.

With a dawning alarm she remembered that Michael knew nothing about Chris Donahue. What with Lindsay being there, then with the house full of people and Michael slaving away in the kitchen, she had never found the right moment.

Panic took over when she tried to imagine what would happen if Michael were to enter the kitchen and stumble, unwarned and unprepared, into the man he had known three years ago as Kane. Too late she opened her mouth to call out and stop him, but at that very moment, Chris stepped out of the kitchen, holding a mug of coffee in his hand, obviously fed up waiting there alone.

Both men stopped as they saw each other and Ariel's hand rose to her mouth when she saw the look of shocked recognition on Michael's face.

'Good Lord, Kane! I don't believe it!' The name came out slightly blurred by sleep and wine, but it sounded deafeningly clear to Ariel. Neither man saw her, standing as she was halfway up the stairs, but she could see Chris's face, half lit by the kitchen light behind him, and she waited, frozen, to see his reaction.

'Did you say Kane?' he asked pleasantly. 'The name is Chris, actually.'

Michael's professional training and quick wit came to her help. It took a fraction of a second for his shocked face to clear, resuming a pleasant, polite surprise, and his voice lost its incredulous edge. 'I beg your pardon,' he said lightly, and Ariel had to grab hold of the railing, almost faint with relief. 'In the half-light, you looked very much like an old friend of mine. I'm Michael Stewart, incidentally. Ariel' brother. I take it you're here on her behalf.'

Chris Donahue stepped forward, transferred the coffee cup to his left hand, and used the other to shak Michael's hand. 'Chris Donahue. How do you do?'

Michael's face registered nothing but a delighte

amazement. 'The computer man? Now, that's a real honour. I had no idea Ariel knew you. Which is rather unfair, don't you think, Ariel?'

His question took her by surprise. She didn't think he had seen her. 'Both Ariel and I are computer freaks,' Michael went on, not waiting for her to collect her wits. 'We tend to compete a little with each other on who's better at cracking the wily bastards but she shouldn't have kept a genius like you all to herself.'

Ariel's laughter came out unnatural and tight. 'You don't share your computerist friends with me, why should I?'

Chris's eyes were moving from her to Michael and back again, listening intently to their light banter, his face impassive.

'Anyway, it has nothing to do with computers,' she went on as her stiff legs took her down the rest of the stairs. 'Chris is the man I've been working for for the last two weeks.' She spoke slowly, deliberately, trying to cram as much information as possible into the least revealing words. 'Adapting his novel into a film script. You remember, I told you all about it . . .'

'Oh, yes, of course,' Michael chimed in. 'Sorry, Sis. What with your endless chatter about anything under the sun, I can't be blamed for not taking it all in, can I?'

The sound of Chris Donahue's chuckle joined in with the brother-sister charade. 'She does talk a lot, doesn't she? Still, I must say, it all makes sense when it comes to scripts. She's good, your sister. Are you busy tonight?'

The question was so unexpected that Michael was thrown off his guard. 'Thank heavens, no. The first free evening in a week. The hospital is short-handed. Flu epidemic, you know.'

'Well, why don't you join us? We're having dinner in town.'

'Oh, no, count me out,' Michael retreated quickly, looking uneasily up at Ariel. 'I was looking forward to an early night.'

Her first reaction was a sharp stab of disappointment. Hard as she tried to convince herself that Chris's surprise visit was the last thing she needed right now, she couldn't help feeling angry and rejected at his quick readiness to include her brother; a total stranger, as far as he was concerned. Unless, she stiffened, her over-strained mind already smelling danger, unless it had to do with Michael's inadvertent slip at addressing him as 'Kane'. It was obviously a plan to pump them both for the truth. Well, let him try, she reasoned with herself. Michael was more than a match for Chris and exactly the kind of protection she needed.

Running down the rest of the stairs, she hurried over to Micahel and put a hand on his arm. 'Oh, please, Michael. Do come,' she pleaded, terrified now of being left alone with Chris, prey to his unavoidable inquisition. 'I'd love it and you can bore Chris all evening with all your computing frustrations and triumphs.'

Chris joined in, assuring Michael that it would save him from spending the evening going over the same old arguments about scene cuts, dissolves and flash-backs which a dinner alone with Ariel would invariably mean. Michael was helplessly trapped. Finally, giving Ariel a bewildered look, he went upstairs to change his jeans and sweat-shirt into more formal clothes.

Left alone in the hall with Chris, Ariel waited rigidly for the inevitable remark about Michael's slip.

'Seems like a nice chap, your brother,' he said pleasantly, unpredictable as ever. 'A psychiatrist, I think you said, is that right?'

'Yes,' she said tightly.

'And a computer freak, as well,' he went on, grinning down at her, his expression dangerously innocent of suspicion or mockery. 'I wonder why you never told him you're working for me.'

Ariel turned away from his assessing blue gaze. 'I didn't want to say anything until I was sure you were going to keep me on.'

'Quite right too,' he congratulated her good sense. 'And now that you know you've got the job . . .'

She broke in, anticipating his next question. 'I didn't have a chance today. We had guests and as you saw for yourself, we all got sloshed.'

'Well, it's a good thing he's coming to dinner with us. This way we can tell him together about flying to the Seychelles on Wednesday.'

She still couldn't tell whether he had heard from Paul or not. 'Look, Chris,' she started, weakly. 'I . . . I don't think I could come with——'

'Ah, Michael. That was quick.' Chris cut her short, turning to greet her brother as he came down the stairs wearing the dark grey suit he usually wore to hospital. 'Shall we go in two cars or what?'

'Lindsay's taken mine, I'm afraid,' Michael explained uneasily.

'We can take my Renault,' Ariel offered quickly. 'That way Chris won't have to drive us back home.'

Chris was already pushing her towards the door. 'Nonsense.' He coolly discarded her suggestion. 'We'll be much warmer and cosier squeezed all together in the Porsche. Get your coat, Ariel.'

The Mayfair restaurant sparkled with an aura of subtle exclusivity and unobstrusive affluence. It was a popular watering-hole among film and theatre folk who always felt protected here from the greedy gapes of star gazing outsiders. It also happened to be Ariel's favourite place. She had been lunched and dined there by producers and story-editors too often to feel intimidated or awed by the proximity of so many famous faces, but tonight, walking in with Chris Donahue, she felt oddly conspicuous and self-conscious.

For all his well-publicised adventures, Chris's face remained unfamiliar to the general public because of his overt dislike for press photographers. Yet, the moment they entered the crowded restaurant, she was uncomfortably aware of the curious looks, particularly those of women, which were directed at him, obviously wondering who that forceful, attractive stranger was. And as his female escort, she was attracting the same subtle, occasionally envious looks which seemed to be assessing her as the mystery man's female escort. Feeling awkward and perversely annoyed, she stepped back, attaching herself to her brother, trying to create the impression that it was Michael she was with.

'Good to see you again, Mr Donahue,' Ronny, the young manager, greeted Chris with reserved pleasure and then turned to her, beaming with a frank, welcoming smile. 'Hello, Ariel. Haven't seen you around here for quite a while.' Bending down, he kissed her cheek which immediately declared her a regular and a welcome customer for the benefit of anyone who didn't know her. Ronny, in his own modest way, was something of a star-maker.

Ariel smiled back, warmed by his friendly greeting, and introduced Michael, and then they were led to a table which Ronny always kept reserved for important late-bookers who couldn't be refused. Like Chris Donahue, in this case.

The evening started out quite harmlessly, lulled by the delicious, light *nouvelle cuisine* feast. She might as well have stayed at home for all the attention she received. Her brother and Chris seemed to have hit it off from the moment they sat down, falling into an animated conversation about computers which was Chris's special genius and quite an obsession with both Michael and herself. Joining in, she began to relax slightly, stupidly forgetting Chris's strategy of numbing his victims' wits with his easy charm until they shed all their defences, and pouncing on them the moment they were completely off guard.

'Tell me about your work, Michael.' Chris turned suddenly on Michael. 'I'm quite fascinated by the hocus-pocus of psychiatry.'

Ariel stiffened, smelling danger. Chris was obviously trying to trap her brother into admitting that he knew about his amnesia. But Michael, far more cunning than she was when it came to the wiles of his fellow-men, just smiled easily. 'What department in particular?' he asked innocently, avoiding the furious darts her eyes were aiming at him.

'Which department is your speciality?' Chris

answered with a question, easily falling in with Michael's dangerous game. In fact, it seemed to her that both men were rather enjoying matching their wits against each other.

Michael didn't hesitate. 'Oh, normal abnormalities, if you know what I mean; dropping-out problems, creative lapses, memory blocks, that sort of thing.' He ignored Ariel's soft gasp. For a moment she thought he would dive straight into Chris's special problem. 'You find a lot of it in London. The rat-race syndrome, you know.'

She breathed in relief as he smoothly led the conversation away from danger. Keeping well within the etiquette of professional discretion, he kept them entertained with light-hearted, amusing stories about presumably normal, ordinary neurosis, which carried them through the main course, the delicious brandy dessert and a good dose of deceptively light Mouton Rothschild vintage which was gradually turning Ariel's alert mind into a drowsy, sluggish mush.

'Well, I could spend all night talking about it,' Michael finally ended his recital over their coffee. 'I've had six long years of it, you know.'

'Six years?' Chris asked, pleasantly. 'I thought you came to England more recently, like Ariel.'

A cold shiver ran down Ariel's back. That was what he had been driving at all evening; he was now going to grill them both about their past, ready to trap Michael into revealing details which she had either faked or carefully kept out. Throwing Michael a warning glance, she barged in, not giving him a chance to answer:

'Oh I came here long after Michael. I made sure he was well settled in the big city so that he'd prepare the ground for me. You know, save me the trouble of making first contacts . . .'

'Social contacts, you mean?' Chris wanted to know, undeceived by her rather blunt attempt to pull the conversation away from St Patrick. 'Is that why you came here, Ariel? To meet people? Were you very lonely in your island?'

To her horror, Michael took over. 'Far too lonely,'

he said calmly, refusing to meet her frantic look. 'Our parents were getting quite worried about her. You see, St Patrick is quite cut off from the rest of the world and we all felt she needed to get out, especially after a prolonged visit of a friend of mine which ended rather unhappily.

'For God's sake, Michael.' Ariel stopped him, her voice rising shrilly. 'I don't think Chris is interested in my life story.'

'I think he is,' her brother corrected her, drily. 'Aren't you, Chris?'

'Of course I am,' was the prompt answer.

Feeling like a trapped animal, she saw the two men exchange looks as if in the short time that they had known each other they had developed a silent, secret language. Uneasily, she let her eyes rove from Chris's handsome, impassive face to Michael's freckled, deceptively boyish one, trying to read the signals which were passing between them, uneasily aware of the empathy between these two highly intelligent and perceptive minds.

'I take it this friend of yours is the famous elusive Kane,' Chris went on after a short pause, and she knew that the question was meant for her even though he was still looking at Michael.

'That's right. The man I mistook you for when we met earlier on,' her brother agreed, affably. 'The resemblance is quite uncanny, don't you agree, Ariel?'

She wanted to hit both of them for treating her most secret, most agonising torment with such a cold, casual disregard. She was used to Chris taunting her with his sardonic remarks, but she could hardly believe that her brother, always so sensitive and considerate of her feelings, could mock her so sadistically.

She stood up, almost toppling the chair over in her angry haste, and grabbed her over-sized shoulder bag. 'I suppose so,' she said coldly. 'Will you excuse me, please?'

She stayed in the luxurious Ladies' Room as long as she dared, trying to curb the flow of her angry tears. But finally she was driven out by the curious, sympathetic looks of the elderly attendant, only to find Chris alone at their table, calmly sipping his Calvados.

'Where is he?' she attacked his grinning handsome face angrily.

'Michael? Oh, he decided to stay in town. Less trouble getting to work tomorrow morning, he said. And that's your Armagnac, incidentally, compliments of Ronny. Your customary after-dinner drink, according to him.'

She looked down on him with open hostility. 'No thanks. I've had enough for one day. And I'd like to go home now, if you don't mind.'

'Certainly.' Chris smiled up at her. 'I'm almost finished. Sit down.'

She remained standing. 'I'd rather take a taxi back home. It's too much out of your way.'

Gently but firmly, he took hold of her arm and pulled her down to her chair. 'Nonsense. Now just sit down and relax. I haven't paid the bill yet.'

A few minutes later, she was sitting beside him in the dark car, squeezed painfully against the door in her effort to keep as great a distance between them as she could in the enclosed capsule. She remained stubbornly silent, trying to keep her fury refuelled as a shield against his disturbing nearness, but she was too exhausted, too dazed with the events of the last two days. All she wanted was to be back home to crawl into bed and drown in sleep.

'I think it's time you delivered your part of the deal,' she heard him say casually, mocking her angry silence, his eyes concentrating on the intricate network of West End streets.

'What deal?' she said sullenly. 'When did I ever make a deal with you?'

'On your first night at the villa, remember? You were to tell me all about that mysterious Kane if I agreed to take you with me to the Seychelles.'

It was a brazen, unfair, arrogant misinterpretation of their conversation. Ariel sat up, bristling with rage. 'Listen, Chris. You can play those games with my brother, you two obviously enjoy this kind of thing, but not with me. I never agreed to anything of the kind.'

He gave her a quick, amused smile. 'Perhaps not, but I would still like to hear about the man whose ghost I keep resurrecting with the most intriguing regularity. Who is he?'

Tiredly, she gave in. 'He's a friend of Michael's and he stayed a few months with us on St Patrick. And you happen to look like him ... a little,' she corrected herself firmly. 'The resemblance is very superficial. No one could mistake you for him after a few seconds of acquaintance.'

'Why?' Chris's voice hardened. 'Where does the difference begin, exactly?'

'Well, for starters, he isn't an arrogant, insufferable and cold-blooded egomaniac,' she spat at him.

'You forgot to add amnesiac to the list,' he murmured drily and she was seized by a hysterical confusion of agony and laughter. She began to feel like a character in a nightmarish farce.

'If he were,' she finally managed to stammer, 'if he were, I certainly wouldn't have held it against him.'

'No, I shouldn't think you would. But the fact remains that whatever he is, you're still keeping yourself for him, even though he hasn't been around for three years.' He kept his eyes on the road but his voice was tight with contempt. 'Don't you think that's carrying loyalty a bit too far?'

'Did Michael tell you that?' she attacked, avoiding his question. 'What else did my "loyal" brother tell you? You seem to have covered quite a lot of ground during the short time I left you two together.'

'Quite,' he agreed, unmoved by her caustic remark. 'We both thought it best, though, to let you supply the details.'

'How very gallant.'

Chris threw her a quick look, his lips curled into that infuriating half-smile. 'Oh, we didn't mean to be gallant. Only practical. As you said, Michael and I had very little time alone together and since you and I are leaving on Wednesday there was no chance of another talk, so ...'

There was no way she could shake him out of his smug indifference to her well-justified indignation. 'Oh, to hell with both of you,' she summed up her disgust, and was flung forward as the Porsche came to a screeching halt.

She had gone too far, she thought, and braced herself to meet his icy anger. But instead, he just leaned over, one hand stretched out towards her. She recoiled away, pushing against the hard door, determined not to let him take her in his arms. But she immediately felt stupidly mortified when his hand just went past her to open the door on her side.

'Get out, Ariel,' he said mildly. 'We're home.'

'Oh, thanks,' she said as coldly as she could, still smarting with embarrassment. 'Sorry I dragged you all the way here and thanks for the dinner. At least the food was great. Good night.'

Instead of answering, he began to open his own door, taking her invitation for a night-cap for granted with a typical smug arrogance. With a renewed surge of apprehension she remembered that Michael wasn't sleeping home tonight.

'Wait, Chris,' she stopped him before he began to walk away towards the house, 'I don't think you should come in. You have quite a long drive back home,' she explained lamely.

'I am home,' he informed her calmly, looking at her with a raised eyebrow. And suddenly aware of the eerie silence, she looked out of the window. There were no rows of detached houses, no ancient lamp-posts, just the shadows of trees looming in the distance through the thick darkness of the Heath and the single lamp which illuminated the front door of Chris's villa.

CHAPTER NINE

AFTER a second of stunned disbelief, she rushed after him, bursting through the door he had left open for her. 'Damn you, Chris Donahue!' she shouted at him, her voice ringing throughout the quiet house. 'You tricked me!'

His face was a dark shadow as he turned to face her. 'Keep your voice down, Ariel. You'll wake them up.'

'I don't care if——' she started to say, and suddenly remembered where she was. The villa was still full of Chris's relatives. She turned back to him, her voice dropping to a furious whisper. 'You knew all along, didn't you? You knew I wasn't coming back here tomorrow, so you tricked me! That's why you came over tonight, wasn't it? And now I don't even have my car with me. God, I could kill you!'

'Not now, darling. You're far too tired and so am I. You can kill me tomorrow. Good night.' He was already going in the direction of his rooms.

'Oh no you don't,' she called out, forgetting to keep her voice down again. 'I've got something to say to you. Now!'

'Can't it wait till the morning?'

'No ... I want it out now,' she shouted, stamping her foot.

Sighing in mock resignation, he came back and stood in front of her, a dark tall shadow, relieved only by the startling glint of his sparkling eyes. 'All right, but not here. You're bound to wake the whole house up and I'd rather not turn this into a family conference.'

With mock gallantry, he pushed open the double doors and bowed her into the dark spacious lounge. Vaguely she realised that this was the first time she had been with him in any other part of the villa outside the study. It felt as strange and unfamiliar as being with him in the crowded restaurant, surrounded by people. How odd, she thought irrelevantly, it had always been just the two of them alone. She had never seen him in a social situation. Their relationship had been just as unreal as it had been with Kane.

She wasn't going to sit down but he pushed her into the deep settee and sat beside her. 'That's better,' he decided warmly. 'Now let's hear what it was you wanted to tell me.'

She took a deep breath. 'I am not going with you. I'm sorry. But it won't work.'

He wasn't impressed. 'So I gathered from Paul this morning. He said it wouldn't be ... seemly, I think was the word he used.' She shuffled uneasily, aware of the amusement behind the cool, grave tone. 'Your brother, on the other hand, didn't seem at all averse to the idea. He actually thinks it would do you a world of good. Sailing again, visiting your parents, that sort of thing.'

His hand, as he spoke, came to rest on her short hair, stroking it back, in a light, avuncular gesture.

Angrily, she pulled her head away. 'Well, it has nothing to do with either Michael or Paul.' She tried to sound cool and unaffected by his touch. 'It's my decision. I just can't afford to leave London for such a long period of time and Paul can easily find you someone else, if you need anyone at all.'

To her dismay, she could feel herself being pulled into the circle of his arms, her feeble attempts to get away utterly ignored. 'But I don't want anyone else,' he said lightly. 'Besides, I need you to give me a guided tour around your Enchanted Island. I'm curious to see the actual location of *The Island of the Lost*.'

'The what?' she whispered, hardly believing her ears.

'St Patrick,' he explained calmly. His fingers moved down to her throat, their touch as light as a feather, as if mildly intrigued by the structure of her bones, the texture of her skin. 'Isn't that the original model for my—our fictitious island?'

He remembers, a voice kept roaring in her ears. He remembers everything. He was Kane again. And yet he was so strange, so detached, so ... yes, so dangerous.

She tried to sit up, but his hand kept her head firmly against the soft sofa cushions, stroking her hair in the same detached, oddly menacing manner. 'How

long have you ...' she started to say after a long
silence, her husky voice hardly audible.

'You mean how long have I known? Oh, almost
from the very start, I guess. You see, I became
extremely intrigued by your astounding familiarity
with my ... with the novel,' he corrected himself
enigmatically. 'But you seemed oddly out of date, far
more at home with my ... with the first, original
version than with the final version on which we were
working. Like, for example, your connecting the
whole thing with *The Tempest* or your assumption that
Alexis was a human being and not a humanoid ...
And various other details which I have discarded,
characters which I have altered, even names.'

She felt faint as the tension left her body, bringing
instead a wave of unspeakable agony. He remembered
nothing. He was still harping on his old suspicions,
trying to trap her into revealing her reasons for
coming after him. And she'd never yet felt so
threatened by him, so vulnerable to the touch of that
relentless, stroking hand.

'So will you tell me now, Ariel, how did you get
hold of the original version?' His hand, still gentle but
now overtly menacing, held her down as she tried to
move. 'And just to save you the trouble of concocting
another ingenious story, let me tell you that the
only existing copy is safely stashed away aboard my
yacht.'

She didn't answer. Even if she could think of an
explanation, she knew he wouldn't believe her.

'At least I managed to stop your flowing imagination. That's something, I suppose. Well, shall I try
and fill in the gaps myself? You remember I told you I
woke up in Mahe with a gaping hole in my memory?
Well, as it happens, the only tangible souvenir I kept
from that lost period of my other life was a briefcase
with a thick wad of typed manuscript. Unfinished but
rather promising, I thought, except for some rather
sentimental quirks. So I began by doctoring it and
somehow went on to finish it, and that's how *The
Island of the Lost* came to be.' He gave a soft,

unamused chuckle. 'I knew that I couldn't have written the damn thing myself, you see, and so it occurred to me that by publishing the novel under my name, bringing it out as a major film, I would smoke the legitimate writer out of his hole. He was bound to rush out, panting to sue the life out of me.'

Ariel was no longer aware of his roving hand. She just gaped at him dumbly, her eyes wide and unblinking. 'And you accuse me of having a rich imagination?' she whispered finally. 'This . . . this is crazy!'

'Not really,' Chris explained, a slight edge to his calm voice. 'If anyone can give me a clue as to who I was and where I had been, it has to be him. Or her, as the case may be.' He paused, and his brilliant gaze came slowly down to hold hers captive. 'So sweetheart, why not admit that it was you?'

'What?' The high, shrill voice couldn't be hers.

He didn't seem at all affected by her shocked reaction. 'It's occurred to me almost from the very first day. There were far too many coincidences, my darling. Your name, your coming from the Seychelles, your familiarity with the original version . . . A five-year-old kid would have started wondering with far less than that. And I'm much older and wiser.'

'Oh, my God, Chris, You . . . you——' Her hand came up to arrest the menacing hand and clinging on to it, she burst out laughing. They seemed to be embroiled in some cruel farce, a proper *Comedy of Errors*. 'I'm sorry,' she gasped in between renewed bursts of laughter. 'I . . . I just can't help it, Chris.'

He didn't find her laughter amusing. His hand came down heavily on her shoulder, squeezing it in a vice-like, painful grip. 'That damned laughter again!' he said softly. 'It all adds up!'

Her laugh died off, cooled by the icy rage she remembered so well. 'Oh, God, I don't know what to say, Chris. It's just too ludicrous.'

'But true. Shall we agree on that?' he said, drily. 'All I need to know now is what lay behind this farce. Why didn't you just come out with it and demand your novel back? I somehow can't believe it was money compensation you were after. It couldn't be me, since you're so obviously hooked on that bloody Kane. So what is it, damn you?' His voice rose finally to a cold, furious pitch and his long fingers closed around her neck, terrifying her with their caressing menace. 'What do you expect to get out of me?'

'You've got it all wrong, all wrong!' she whispered hoarsely back at him. 'How could you go on working with me all this time if that's what you had on your mind?'

'I could ask you the same question. Now, tell me the truth before I strangle it out of you!'

'It's ... it's Kane,' she blurted out, the words coming out before she could think. 'Kane wrote it.'

As if she had used a magic word, her neck was suddenly free of his relentless hold, and the twisted mouth, which a moment ago was scathing her skin with its breath, withdrew. All she could see now was the shadowy outline of his broad shoulders and the proud lines of his profile. She remained quite still afraid to remind him of her existence by moving, the silence plucking at her nerves as if they were overstrained guitar strings.

'Kane again,' he murmured, finally breaking the silence. 'Whichever way I look, I seem to be living off the bastard's left-overs.'

With a disgusted grunt, he pushed her away and stood up. Then, struck by another thought, he looked down again, his eyes glinting angrily. 'So, when can I expect the doubtful honour of meeting him? I now owe him a triple debt: his novel, his film and ...' he hesitated for a second, 'and his girl. How long do I have to wait before he comes to collect his due?'

'I wouldn't hold my breath, Chris,' she answered wearily. 'Kane won't be coming back. Ever.'

He stared at her. 'So he *is* dead, then?'

Ariel shook her head. That was one lie she couldn't bring herself to utter. 'Good,' he muttered, more to himself than to her. 'At least he's left me the small pleasure of killing him myself.'

In a few long strides, he reached the door and then turned back, his voice still low and menacing. 'You'd better face facts, Ariel. Like it or not, you're coming with me to the Seychelles and don't delude yourself that we'll be spending any more time on the script adaptation. Let Kane finish it now. He's welcome to the novel, the script and the money. I'll settle for his girl.'

'Well, I won't!' she cried as she rushed after him into the hall. 'I don't want you as a substitute and I won't be one myself. You can't make me, Chris!'

He was rigid with cold fury as he turned on her. 'I can and I will, Ariel. For your sake as well as mine. We have to get rid of the ghosts and I'm your chance to do so just as you are mine. We'll just have to try and live together, enjoy each other's bodies and perhaps, one day, we may even learn to love each other.'

Her outrageous cry was muffled by his angry, determined kiss. And then the hall was flooded with light and she suddenly found herself, still clasped tightly in Chris's hands, but looking straight into Cynthia's green eyes.

'How sweet.' The model's liquid voice was tight with rage. 'How long do you intend to carry on with her, Chris? Until the adaptation is over or was that supposed to be a farewell kiss?'

Chris was already walking away, leaving both women behind to sort things between themselves.

'Chris!' Cynthia shrieked, her voice losing its mellow honey warmth. 'I want to know where I stand with you!'

He turned around. 'Oh, is that all? Well, that's easy enough.' He made a few steps towards her, his face taking on that pleasant, blank expression which Ariel knew pre-empted the worst kind of assault from him. 'I thought I made that clear enough long before you married Gordon.'

'But I left him for you,' the woman hissed, sullenly.

'I never asked you to. I told you then as I'm telling you now, I don't want you, Cynthia. And if this still hasn't sunk in let me try another one on you. We're getting married, probably next week, in the Seychelles.' Both women were gaping at him, stupidly. 'And in case there's still some uncertainty in either of your minds, by "we" I meant myself and Ariel, of course. Good night.'

Seeing Cynthia's lovely face distorted with frustrated rage and genuine agony, she forgot for a moment her own shaken incredulity at the sadistic cruelty of his heartless joke and tried to force her stunned brain to come up with words which would soothe the distraught beauty. 'Please, Cynthia, you mustn't take him seriously,' she cleared her parched throat. 'He didn't mean it. He was just teasing us. Me as well as you. You must believe me.'

Cynthia didn't seem to hear her. For a moment it looked as if she was going to attack her physically and Ariel stepped back, her hand outstretched to ward off the oncoming blow. But the woman just stood there, her green eyes brimming with helpless tears, and the next moment she vanished into the darkness of the bedroom corridor.

The sound of a door being slammed with desperate viciousness echoed through the air and then the house sank back into silence.

Still numb with the shock of his parting words, Ariel dragged her weary feet towards the bedroom which only this morning she had been determined never to see again. Except that now she could only think of that resolution with bitter mockery. She had been a fool to think that she could get away from Chris Donahue. Nothing would stop him from forcing her to come with him. He believed that she held the key to the mystery of his past and he was determined to use her. And she knew now that even when she screamed her denials, she had already accepted the inevitable. She was his, whether he loved her or not.

She was about to switch on the light in her bedroom when the sound of deep, steady breathing made her stop just in time. Evidently, Grace had taken advantage of her absence and offered her bedroom to some out-of-town guest.

With weary resignation, she withdrew, closing the door as gently as she could behind her and stood, undecided in the dark corridor, trying to think what to do next. It was no use trying any of the other bedrooms in this part of the house since she had a very strong suspicion that all of them would be occupied tonight. The only solution would be to make a bed for herself in one of the lounges, except that she had no idea where Marjorie kept the bed-linen and the blankets. The study was the only room which seemed small and cosy enough and in the least danger of being invaded in the morning by the marauding Donahues.

She tiptoed back to the main hall, picked up her warm coat and made her way to the study. It was cold, the central heating having been turned off for the night, and she had no idea how to shut the row of louvred slits along the glass wall which Marjorie had left open for circulation. Looking down on her immensely creasable linen dress, she decided to take it off, leaving on her bra and skimpy briefs, and tucking her large coat around her, she settled as comfortably as she could in the springy depth of Chris's Eames lounger and waited for sleep to relieve her from the bewildering turmoil of the last few hours.

She was floating in the air, light and weightless, her head resting against something warm and vibrating, hard yet giving. She was dreaming, of course; just another variation of a recurring dream. And she knew better than to open her eyes and let reality shatter the blissful illusion of her contentment.

The floating sensation lasted far too short a time. With a protesting moan, she felt her body being lowered down to rest against the more prosaic surface of a bed. But the soft flutter of warm, firm lips against her forehead assured her that she was still drifting securely in the realm of her dream. Feeling safe now, she opened her eyes.

'Why are you still dressed?' she mumbled, vaguely bemused and still steeped in the sweet illusion of her dream. She raised her hand and started to unbutton his shirt. Her hand was slapped away, good naturedly.

'I wouldn't do that, Ariel,' she heard Kane's soft chuckle. 'I'm just as sleepy as you are but don't push your luck.'

Something was beginning to tug at her senses but she clung tenaciously to her drowsy bliss.

The bed sagged slightly under the weight of his body as he stretched beside her, leaving a huge gap between them for some odd reason. But Ariel, with a sigh of utter contentment, snuggled comfortably against his chest, burying her head, as she always did, in the hollow under his shoulder. But instead of being cradled in Kane's arms she was pushed firmly away as Chris's dry, unamused voice jarred her drowsy senses. 'Stop it, Ariel! Just stay on your side of the bed. The idea was sleep not having fun.'

'What are you doing here?' Her voice was husky with sleep but her body, as she sat up, horribly awake.

'Trying to sleep,' Chris answered, coolly. 'This is my bed, in case you haven't noticed.'

Her eyes could dimly discern some looming outlines of strange objects; she was in a room she had never seen before. 'How did I get here then?'

He groaned and raised himself on one elbow, studying her indignant expression. 'I found you sleeping in the study. You didn't look terribly comfortable, moaning and muttering and shivering with cold. So I brought you here. What, if I may ask, was the idea of camping there?'

'Someone's sleeping in my bed,' she said sulkily.

'Poor little Baby Bear,' Chris chuckled and she joined him reluctantly, as she registered the familiar nursery-story words she had uttered. 'Which Goldilocks was it?'

'I've no idea. I didn't stop to investigate,' she answered caustically, throwing off the covers and struggling out of bed.

'Probably Daria. You should have woken her up.'

She refused to be pacified by his casual easy chat. 'Thank you for being so considerate but you really shouldn't have bothered,' she announced, walking towards the door. 'I was really quite comfortable in the study . . . Oh, hell!' she broke in mid-sentence as a gust of cold air made her aware, far too late, of her half-naked state. With a furious groan she hurried back to the bed, clumsily gathering the discarded blankets around her.

'Where's . . . where are my clothes?' she said drily against his soft laughter.

'I don't know. Where you left them, I guess. But your coat is on the floor here somewhere.'

Angrily, she pulled at the blanket, meaning to wrap it around her so that she could get out of bed again without exposing herself to his mocking eyes. But the blanket wouldn't budge. Chris, fully dressed, was lying on top of it.

'That's done it.' Chris was chuckling now, his voice, Kane's disturbingly warm voice sending dangerous shivers down her spine. 'I'm afraid I've changed my mind about you staying on your side of the bed. Your first instinct was, as usual, far more astute than mine. Come here, then.'

'Don't!' she hissed furiously, her legs and hands clumsily flaying at him as he was pulling her to him. 'Damn you, Chris, let me go!'

'Why? Only a minute ago you snuggled into me as if my shoulder were your natural habitat.'

She was too busy resisting her own hunger to think of an answer. Her arms were imprisoned by the relentless grip of his one hand, while one long, muscular leg pinned her knees down to the bed, rendering her completely powerless; all she could do was move her head frantically from side to side to avoid his mouth.

'Stop fighting it, Ariel.' He wasn't laughing any more, his voice was low and steady but there was a tense edge to it. 'Your body seems quite happy to use mine as a substitute, so why deny it since I'm more than willing?'

'No!' she almost shouted.

With a soft angry curse, he captured her head with two hard hands, forcing it to receive his mouth as it came swooping down to penetrate hers with punishing cruelty. Helplessly trapped now, she made her body go rigid, desperately pleading with her inner self not to respond to the invasion of his tongue, to his angry, hurting hands which kept roving down her back, her thighs, the length of her legs and back again, impatiently pushing away the flimsy barriers of her bra and brief bikini pants which impeded their blind reacquaintance with what they had once known with such intimate love.

It was hopeless. She was betrayed by her senses, by her foolish love, by her exhausted will-power. Her body was transmitting the unmistakable messages of her surrender which Chris was quick to register in spite of his angry impatience. Relaxing against her now still body, he rolled slightly to his side, the angry, punishing exploration of his hands mellowing into a slow, sensual caress, his hard lips softening to engulf her mouth, the tip of his tongue coaxing her desire with a light but confident persistence. And as the sweet agony of her aroused passion flowed from the pit of her stomach throughout her lifeless limbs, she no longer wanted to control her need for him.

'That's right, darling, let it happen,' he whispered into her hair, his warm breath sending shivers throughout her body. 'It's time you started living again. Kane is gone, Ariel.'

For a second she was suspended in a state of utter stillness as his words registered, and then she tore herself away from his intoxicating embrace, burying her head in the pillows. 'Oh, go away, Chris,' she sobbed in exasperation mingled with misery. 'It's all so hopeless.'

Her shoulders were seized by two firm hands and she was cradled against Chris's broad, hard chest, her tears staining the crisp cool fabric of his shirt. 'Nothing is hopeless, my love,' he said softly. 'Nothing except your loyalty to Kane. He's gone, Ariel. But I'm here.'

A tiny flame of incredulous hope leapt to life. She couldn't mistake the shades of loving yearning, the aching hunger in the soft murmur, and she tried to raise her head so that she could see his face, reassure herself that she hadn't just imagined it. But his strong hands refused to let go, clasping her head tighter against his thudding heart. 'Keep still, darling,' he murmured. 'Just let me love you.'

She sagged against him, faint with the sudden explosion of a joy she had utterly despaired of ever finding again. Her reason was still trying to warn her not to trust that unbearable surge of hope, but as his lips came down to find hers in a soft, giving kiss and his arms cradled her with that old protective love, she banished all doubts and drowned herself tremblingly in the mindless bliss of her budding happiness. She was home at last. He loved her. Chris loved her.

She was the girl of St Patrick again, utterly uninhibited, secure in the knowledge of his total love for her, moaning with escalating impatience as his calm, soothing hands resumed their slow, confident journey of rediscovery, responding to her unspoken needs with the confidence of past intimacy.

She started to fumble with the buttons of his shirt, her fingers hungry for the hard, warm wall of his naked chest so long denied her. And when at last her lips could savour again the intoxicating texture of his smooth skin, she reached under the loose shirt, loving the feel of the muscles as they contracted and rippled with the pleasure of her caressing hands as they ran down his stomach, pushing beyond the restricting belt of his trousers.

And then she felt his body go rigid.

For a timeless moment everything stood still and a vague inexplicable terror gripped her stomach as he wrenched himself from her clinging hands and stood above her. The room was suddenly flooded in the soft light of the bedside lamp and she shut her eyes against it.

'Oh no,' she whispered. 'Don't go away again. Please!'

'Go away?' Kane's voice, warm and intimate, caressed her. 'I just want to see you when I love you, Ariel.'

Nothing could sound more natural than the words he had just uttered with such loving, familiar intimacy as past and present, Kane and Chris merged into one entity. She had no idea what had brought on that momentary withdrawal but seeing the intense look in the dark blue eyes she knew that he was hers. Whether Kane or Chris, he loved her.

Unhurriedly he removed his shirt then turned to her to relieve her of her bra and her briefs, his eyes travelling over her naked body with slow, deliberate delight.

He smiled with loving amusement as her arms came to pull him to her. 'Wait, darling. Haven't you learnt yet not to rush me?'

'I don't care!' she laughed up at him. 'I only know that I love you so much I'm afraid I'll burst.'

He responded to her flowing, unguarded cry with a strangled groan, and stretching on the bed beside her, he crushed her in his arms, moulding her shape into his. The long years which had separated them melted away as her body, impatient with its passive role as the receiver of pleasure, burnt with the savage urge to give back, to arouse the same uncontrollable shudders in that masterful masculine body, to delight in her power to make his muscles tighten with an unexpected thrill, to force out of that proud mouth involuntary gasps of pleasure. And at last she felt her thighs gripped tightly by two steely hands as a smooth, muscled thigh pushed her legs apart. And she arched her back to receive him, crying out his name.

She was too steeped in her ecstatic anticipation of his thrust to notice the sudden stillness which seemed to grip Chris's being, the slackening hold of his hands on her thighs, the dead weight of his immobile body as it sagged on top of her.

'Open your eyes, Ariel,' he ordered, ignoring her protesting whimper. 'Look at me.'

Trustingly, she forced her eyes open, as she had always done, to let him gaze into her depth, offering her love freely, openly, knowing that now like always before there were no barriers between them. And then, as if drenched by a jet of icy water, she knew that she had lost him again.

It was that certain look on his face which penetrated her delirious senses, transporting her with a sickening jolt of recurring despair to another time and another place, where she saw the same brilliant dark blue eyes burrow into hers with such naked pain. It was the last time Kane had held her in his arms, the day they said goodbye in the palm-leaf shed. The day before he went away to safeguard her from what he considered his unworthy love.

'Oh no, God, not again!' The words came brokenly out of her parched lips. 'Oh, please, Chris. You don't understand . . .' And despairing of expressing herself, she pulled his head down, trying to salvage their love with her kiss, to obliterate the agony of farewell with the power of her emotions.

His mouth refused to respond. Gently, he pulled himself out of her arms, to lie, breathing heavily, beside her. His hand came to wipe the tears which were flowing down her cheeks, and then he relented and raised his head to touch her lips with a soft, infinitely gentle and resigned kiss.

'You were right, darling. We're still not ready for each other,' he said softly, his eyes holding on to hers. 'I don't suppose you can help loving Kane any more than I can help loving you.'

She was sobbing brokenly now. 'But it's you I love,' she tried to tell him. 'You, Chris!'

He said nothing for a long time, his hands comforting her absently. 'It was Kane you cried for.'

She tried to speak, to protest, but his hand came to rest on her mouth. 'Hush, darling. I don't think I can bear to hear any more about Kane right now. Go to sleep now. We can talk about it all day tomorrow.'

Hugging her to him, he kept stroking her, soothing her shuddering sobs until he felt her body go limp, and at last could hear her shallow, calm breathing as she sank into sleep, like an exhausted child. For a long time he held her in his arms, his eyes staring at the curtained window, noting the chink of light as it grew brighter with the coming of dawn, and then, gently, he withdrew from her side and disappeared into his dressing-room.

CHAPTER TEN

SHE woke up in a strange room, drenched in bright sunlight, her heavy, puffed eyes encountering with foggy bewilderment the sparkling green curves of the Heath, stretching beyond the uncurtained patio doors. She raised her head and the slight movement sent a wave of dull pain from the back of her neck down her heavy, aching limbs. Her forehead was damp and hot to the touch. There was no doubt about it. She must have caught a bad cold. With a groan, she sank back against the pillows and tried to shut her mind to some vague nagging terror which was lurking somewhere in the pit of her stomach.

But then she sat up with a jolt as the plump silhouette of Marjorie stepped into her view. 'You'd better get up before the others find you in here, Miss Ariel.' The Irish housekeeper's voice was dry, her eyes refusing to meet Ariel's. 'Here, put this on. I found it in the study.'

Putting Ariel's discarded dress on the bed, she turned her back, and started tidying up the room, tactfully allowing the girl to cover her naked body unobserved.

Her legs almost buckled under as she tried to stand up, and her head seemed to burst with the pounding ache, but leaning against the wall, she managed to get dressed.

'I . . . someone was asleep in my room.' Her mouth was horribly dry, and her voice was hoarse and croaky as she tried to break the embarrassed silence. 'So I . . . I mean, Chris—Oh, what's the use . . .' She gave up on her stammering effort to explain herself. 'I'm sorry, Marjorie. I don't know what to say.'

The disapproving back seemed to relax. 'Oh, don't

feel bad about it, dear.' Marjorie spoke over her shoulder. 'It's quite all right. I'm just a silly old-fashioned woman. You mustn't mind me.'

Ariel sank down to sit on the bed, her legs refusing to hold her. And Marjorie, with a quick, understanding look, walked over to a square, low table by the patio doors, and picked up a cup of tea which she must have left there before drawing the blinds. 'Here, pet. Why don't you drink your tea and then you can go back into the house through the patio. Nobody will see you. They're all in the dining-room, having their breakfast.'

'Where is . . .' she began to stammer. 'Have you seen Chris this morning?'

'He's been out since very early. Jogging around the Heath, I shouldn't wonder.'

The hot tea was beginning to clear away the horrid, stale taste in her mouth, somewhat soothing her aching limbs. In a way, she was almost relieved that she was caught in Chris's bed by Marjorie. It was easier worrying about Marjorie's sensibilities than having to face Chris or to think about the events of the night.

Marjorie's voice reached her again, warm and affectionate now. 'Before any of them start on you, dear, I'd like to tell you that I couldn't be happier about you and Mr Chris. I knew from the very first day you came here, that you were right for him.'

A hot blush covered Ariel's pale cheeks. 'Oh, but it's not like that at all, Marjorie. I mean, you mustn't draw conclusions just because you found me . . . I mean——'

Marjorie giggled at her happily. 'Now, come on, my girl. After all, you'll be married by the end of the week, so there's no need to blush like that.'

'Married?' She raised her voice in shocked astonishment. 'Oh, Marjorie, listen! You've got it all wrong. . . .' She struggled to convey the facts of modern life to the incredibly naive Irish woman.

'Not at all,' the woman assured her. 'Mr Chris told me on Saturday. Just after you left the house. And they all know about it now. So there's no need to keep it a secret.'

Her delighted giggle was joined by a breathless, silvery ripple of laughter. 'You should have seen Cynthia's face when she broke the news to us this morning.' Ariel whirled to face Daria who was beaming at her from the doorway. 'And my poor mother's . . .'

At last she understood. Cynthia had taken Chris's taunting remark of the previous night as an established fact and announced it to the rest of the family. As far as they were concerned, then, she and Chris were now engaged to be married.

What followed next was a nightmare. Utterly dazed by the cruel joke Chris had played on her, she was dragged out of the room, a witless puppet in Daria's enthusiastic hands, and swept into the dining-room, where she was greeted by a chorus of congratulations and introduced to at least half a dozen strangers, all members of the Donahue clan.

Even if she had been able to collect her wits long enough to find words to deny their ridiculous assumptions about her marriage to Chris Donahue, she wasn't given a chance. All her stammered protests were rejected by the falsely hearty welcome of her supposedly future relatives. Cynthia was absent. She had left soon after she told them the news.

Groggy with fever, her head throbbing with pain, Ariel was aware of Grace Donahue's timid smiles, her pathetic attempts to redeem her previous supercilious attitude which were defeated again and again by her husband's sardonic reminders. He himself refrained from any overt declaration of delight, but something in his sheepish smile and cryptic remarks seemed to say that he was more than relieved by the news of his cousin's marriage.

'I knew you'd be the one person in the world to drum some sense into his head,' she heard him say though her mind seemed incapable of absorbing his meaning. 'I hope you'll make him drop that writing nonsense and bring him back to civilisation. He's left me to cope with that empire of his far too long.'

It was Daria who finally saved her. 'Chris's on the

phone, Ariel,' she announced cheerfully, her high clear voice rising about the artificial din. 'He wants to talk to you.'

Stunned, she turned to look at her saviour. 'On the phone? Isn't he here?'

'Apparently not,' Neville answered. 'He left at the crack of dawn. He woke me up with that damned Porsche of his. Go on, darling. Don't keep him waiting.'

Dragging her aching feet to the main hall, she picked up the phone. 'Chris?' she croaked.

'Yes.' There was a short bemused pause. 'Are you all right, Ariel?'

She didn't bother to answer. 'What ... why ... they've all gone mad, Chris. They think you and I ...' She hardly knew what she was saying, but the sound of his voice, the knowledge that he was there, was beginning to soothe her unconscious dread. 'Where are you, Chris?'

'At Heathrow airport,' the voice came clear and steady. 'I'm about to leave.'

'For the Seychelles?'

'No, Ariel. Somewhere else, where you can't find me. I want you to forget all about me.'

'No.' She tried to reach him, but her voice was hardly audible. 'Oh Chris, don't leave! Not again!'

There was a pause at the other end. 'I must, my love. I can't compete with a ghost. Just forget you ever knew me and wait for Kane. He'll be back. I know he'll come back for you ...'

'Chris!' She was clutching the receiver with desperation. 'What about the script, your novel ...'

'Give them to Kane when you meet him again. Goodbye, Ariel.'

She was holding on to the dead receiver until it was removed, almost by force, by Daria. Anxiously, the young girl put an arm around her, supporting her on her weak legs. 'What's wrong, Ariel? Aren't you well?'

Ariel extracted her arm from the younger girl's insistent pull. 'Oh, God, I can't bear this any longer,' she mumbled, making for the door.

Daria was rushing after her, terrified by the odd pallor, the haunted look in the large hazel eyes. 'What's the matter, Ariel?'

'I must get away from here. You've all gone mad.'

She rushed out of the house, making straight to the garage, Daria chasing after all, calling her name.

The Renault wasn't there. Of course. It was still in Dulwich. Chris had brought her here in his car, and then . . . she reeled under the unbearable stab of pain as the memories of last night's events came flooding in.

'What is it, Ariel?' Daria was asking anxiously behind her.

She didn't answer. 'Have you got a car, Daria?' The girl nodded, dumbly. 'May I borrow it? Please, I've got to get away from here!'

The girl looked at her bemusedly. 'I'd better drive you myself,' she said, soberly. 'Let me just tell them——'

'No! I'll get a taxi somewhere . . . I've got to be alone. Let go of me, Daria!'

But Daria held on. 'Chris will kill me if I let you go in such a state. Come on!' And without further argument, she took Ariel firmly by the arm and led her to the small sports Mazda which was parked just outside the villa's front door. 'Get in, Ariel!'

She drove in silence until they left Highgate, giving Ariel time to calm down.

'You didn't know, did you?' she asked when she was sure Ariel was no longer seized by that blind panic. 'He never asked you to marry him, did he?' Ariel shook her head. 'I'm sorry, Ariel. I shouldn't have dragged you through that charade. It just never occurred to me that Chris was just teasing Cynthia.'

'Teasing her!' Ariel's hard laughter sounded strange even to her own ears.

'He must have done it to get her off his back once and for all,' Daria said, thoughtfully. 'He's been telling her for years that he had no intention of getting involved with her again, but this is the first time she seemed to take it seriously. She looked so bewildered

when she told us about it this morning, I had to feel
sorry for her.'

'And you all believed her?'

'Well, yes. We were hardly surprised. Neville and I
have been expecting it for some time now.'

'But Marjorie.' Ariel was shaking her head in
disbelief. 'Marjorie should have known better. How
could she have been taken in by it?'

'Good Heavens, Ariel.' Daria sat up alerted by a
new thought. 'It just occurred to me that . . . Listen,
when I rushed to the kitchen to tell her the news, she
laughed and said that she knew all about it. Chris had
told her himself on Saturday night.'

Ariel gaped at her. 'Saturday night?'

'Yes. So you see, he must have been serious. He
wouldn't mind making fools of Cynthia or of us, but
never of Marjorie. Oh God, isn't it just like Chris!'
The girl started to laugh in relief. 'I guess he just took
it for granted that you'd say yes and never even
bothered to tell you first.' She turned her eyes on the
silent girl beside her, trying to coax a smile out of her.
'Come on, Ariel. I know he's infuriating and all that,
but as long as he wants you, it doesn't really matter,
does it? Oh, I feel so relieved!'

Ariel sank back into the car seat, shutting her eyes.
So it wasn't just a cruel joke, after all. Remembering
the look of agonised love she had caught in his eyes the
night before, she couldn't doubt now that he had
really meant it when he said they were getting
married. It wasn't just a spur-of-the-moment im-
provisation to taunt her and Cynthia with. And the
horrible irony of her predicament, of their mutual
predicament, struck her again. It made no difference
now. Whatever plans Chris might have had the day
before, he was gone now. Leaving the field clear for
Kane, he said. And yet, last night . . . She couldn't
have mistaken the words he had uttered, the way he
looked at her, touched her. She was so certain, so
blissfully sure that he had finally remembered who he
was, that Kane and Chris had at last become one.
Questions, fragments of memories, hopes, despair,

everything was whirling madly in her fuzzy, thick mind increasing the dull, pounding ache inside her head.

'Wake up, Ariel. Please, you've got to wake up. I don't know what to do with you. You're burning with fever.'

The clear, high-pitched voice finally registered. The car wasn't moving any more. Painfully, Ariel opened her eyes, to see Daria's anxious look studying her. 'What?' She could barely speak.

'You're ill,' the girl was saying. 'I think I should take you back to the villa, or to the nearest hospital. I'm so helpless about these things . . .'

She was shivering with cold, but her face was damp with perspiration. She was sick. It wasn't just the shock and the pain. She wished the debilitating headache would go, for just a second, so that she could think straight. But her mind felt like sticky cotton-wool. 'Michael,' she croaked. 'My brother will know what to do.'

'Where is he? Where can we find him?' Poor Daria's voice was shrill with anxiety.

She tried to give Daria Michael's hospital address but she couldn't hear the words coming out. She was slowly being dragged down into a black well of mindless peace, and finally gave in, sinking gratefully into oblivion.

It was fully five days later when she surfaced into full consciousness, to find herself in a private room in Michael's hospital, too weak and numb to feel anything but utter apathy. She had no recollection of how she got into hospital, had no idea how Daria had managed to find her brother. She didn't care much either. All she wanted was to sink back into that blissful delirious state, where she knew no agony, nothing of that dull pain of utter despair which began to creep in as soon as her fever dropped.

People came to see her, ignoring her silent plea to be left alone. Michael and Lindsay more than most, but also Paul Andrews and Dinah, his wife, Daria, who managed with great difficulty to curb her bubbling energy, Marjorie too, even Grace and Neville. But never Chris. He was gone, she kept reminding herself. He told her to forget all about him and went away. For good.

It was pneumonia, Michael told her, having waited until she was well enough to be scolded. 'You seemed perfectly all right when I last saw you at the restaurant. Where the hell did you manage to contract it?'

She shrugged, passively. Vaguely she remembered the few hours she had spent in the cold study, huddled half naked under her thin coat before Chris found her there, 'moaning and shivering with cold' as he explained later, in his bed.

'I ended up in Chris's villa that night,' she reminded him, too apathetic and numb to feel any anger at the way he had deserted her then. 'And my room was occupied so I had to spend the night, camping on a chair, in a rather cold room.'

Michael looked at her, a little sheepishly. 'I'm sorry we gave you such a rough time at the restaurant, pet. But believe me, I knew what I was doing. And so did Kane, or rather, Chris. Why didn't you tell him the truth?'

Ariel turned her head away. She didn't want to talk about either Kane or Chris.

'Come on, Ariel. We must talk about it.' He waited a few seconds. 'All right, then. I don't really need to ask. You didn't want to be loved on credit, is that it? He had to fall in love with you all over again. You thought he'd feel obliged to take you back, sort of paying a debt from his forgotten past. Am I right?' He waited for her to contradict him, but she remained passive, refusing to meet his eyes. 'Well, sister, I must say I'm rather proud of you. Though I should have thought you trusted me enough to share it with me. You always have done, until now.'

'It was unfair of you,' she muttered. 'Once I managed to get that job with him, I decided it was time I carried the burden on my own shoulders.' She chuckled, mirthlessly. 'I almost died when you and he met in the hall. I had meant to tell you about him over the weekend, but . . .'

'I know. There was hardly an appropriate moment.' He took a deep breath, looking somewhat relieved. 'Well, why the miserable face now, then? You got what you wanted. You made him fall in love all over again. He remembers nothing of Ariel of St Patrick. All he cares about is you, a strange girl who has just walked into his life. When you left us alone, he practically asked me for your hand. It was I who suggested that he said nothing and just whizzed you off to the Seychelles.'

'You did?' At last she turned to face him, her eyes dull with pain. 'Why?'

'Because you would have refused.' He smiled at her frowning bemusement. 'You see, pet, he still hasn't realised that he loves you as deeply as Kane did. Because somewhere in his unconscious memory, he still clings to the love he had for another Ariel. You both need to be together alone, for a good long period, before you can crack his stubborn loyalty, make him relinquish his love for that ghost through his new love for you, or until . . .'

'Until what?' she prompted, sardonically, anticipating his answer. 'Until he regains his memory, is that what you were going to say?'

'That's right.'

She sagged back against the pillow. 'He never will, Michael. It's hopeless.'

'You're wrong. He's on the verge. I knew it almost as soon as I saw him. His reaction to me, his questions, the way he was manipulating the conversation . . . He knew we'd met before, Ariel. Not clearly, not enough to remember my face, but it was there. And I'm sure that S Patrick will revive more memories. As long as neither o you pushes too hard. It must happen slowly, gradually That's the best way.'

Ariel stopped listening. 'You don't understand Michael. He thinks I'm in love with another man With Kane.'

She felt a tiny spark of anger when he responded with an amused chuckle. 'He's jealous of Kane! Come on, Ariel. You must admit, it is rather funny, don't you think?'

'I don't think so,' she answered listlessly. 'He's left me, Michael. He said I should forget all about him and wait for Kane to come back for me.'

At last she saw a cloud of perplexed concern dim her brother's boyish grin. 'Left you? I thought he was waiting for you in the Seychelles. We cabled him the day you were brought here, telling him you were ill and would join him later.'

'Did you get any reply?'

There was a long pause. 'No,' he said finally.

'He isn't in the Seychelles. He's gone somewhere I can't find him. That's what he said on the phone, just before he took off.'

For a few moments, the small hospital room was shrouded in silence. And then she heard Michael mutter something unintelligible to himself.

'I don't think I want to talk about it any more, Michael,' she said before he could torment her with any more optimistic illusions. 'Chris is gone and Kane is buried. And that's that.'

Paul Andrews came to see her the day before she left hospital. He had great news for her, he said. Before leaving, Chris Donahue had instructed him to let her finish the script adaptation alone. 'You're also getting a full credit, not to mention the incredible fee. When do you think you can get back to work?'

The mere mention of the script was enough to throw her into a frenzy. She couldn't face any of it. In fact, she couldn't bear the idea of going back to work. All she wanted was to huddle into herself, try and forget Chris.

Michael got her out of this one. Ariel was in no shape to take on any work whatsoever for a while, he said firmly.

'You mean, I have to get her out of all her commitments?' Paul barked, his hand rising to tear his thin hair with a typical gesture of exasperation. 'How the hell do you expect me to do that?'

'You'll find a way,' Michael said calmly. 'Sorry, Mr Andrews, but Ariel is going back home. She needs a few months to recuperate.'

'Home?' A pale spark of pleasure battled valiantly against Ariel's apathy. 'You mean, home to St Patrick?'

'That's right. And don't try to wriggle out of it, Ariel. Doctor's orders.'

She didn't try nor wish to oppose him. She could think of no better place to lick her wounds than the peaceful haven of her island, which held nothing but cherished memories of a happiness which she had lost for ever.

CHAPTER ELEVEN

JULIAN and Laura Stewart were at the airport to greet her, trying not to show how distressed they were by her pale, lifeless face. Somehow they seemed reluctant to take her straight to St Patrick, insisting on a nice welcome lunch at one of the island's exclusive hotels, and then suggesting they went to the club, to meet all her old friends. But to this Ariel objected firmly. She wanted to go home.

Her parents exchanged an odd look, and she saw her father shrug his shoulders resignedly as he started leading his wife and his daughter towards the small inter-island harbour, where a beautiful and gigantic yacht was waiting to take them back.

'What's this, Daddy?' She turned to her father. 'You haven't sent old *Laura* to graze, have you?'

'Not yet, but she's had her day, I'm afraid. I dare say you'll get to like this new one just as much, once you get used to her.'

'And you named her after me?' she smiled at him, trying to summon the energy to make a show of her appreciation. 'I'm really honoured, Daddy. Now, shall we go home?'

The sun was beginning to set when they left

Victoria behind them. And letting her father manipulate the new, dauntingly luxurious yacht, she sat quietly on the deck beside her mother and fixed her eyes on the distant hills of St Patrick, a dim sense of peace beginning to spread throughout her being as the pointed shapes grew larger and nearer, their grey outlines filtering through the hazy air, becoming sharper and greener. And then, she was astonished to feel something close to excitement as she caught the first view of the encircling belt of startlingly white sand against the luscious dark green of the palms and tacamaca trees, already washed in the pink-golden light of the slowly setting sun.

A sharp, brilliant dart blinded her for a second, a reflection of the pink twilight rays as they hit an invisible window. She turned to smile delightedly at her mother as her childhood home, the old Stewart plantation house, was beckoning at her from beyond the thick green curtain of shrubs and trees.

The shed and the house disappeared from view as the yacht made its cautious way into the small bay, its usual mooring place. *Laura*, her faithful old yacht, was rocking gently against the wooden pier, looking even more battered than Ariel remembered. But at least she was still allowed to rest in her usual place; *Ariel*, the usurper, was given the secondary, less convenient mooring spot, usually reserved for visiting yachts.

As if she had never left the island, she took over from her father, safely seeing the new strange yacht home, throwing the anchor just behind poor old *Laura*, then lighting across to the pier to secure her further. She would have swum ashore if she hadn't been hampered by her London clothes.

'You take your time,' she called over to her parents. 'I just can't wait to feel that sand under my feet.'

'No, Ariel!' Laura stopped her as she was about to dash across the pier towards the sandy beach. 'Wait,' please. We must tell you something.'

'Later.' She smiled at her mother's oddly perturbed expression.

She had overestimated her strength. Her illness had left her stupidly weak, and after a few steps, she had to slow down and continue at a more leisurely pace.

Laura and Julian had no trouble catching up with her.

'Ariel,' her mother started, haltingly. 'I don't know how to tell you this, but I must do so before we get to the house. You ... that is, we have a guest staying with us.'

Ariel groaned. 'Oh, what a pity. I hoped I'd have you and the island all to myself for a little while. I hardly expected any guests at this time of year.'

'It's not exactly a guest,' her father barged in. 'It's ...' And his voice trailed off as his eyes strayed to the far end of the beach, where a tall bare-chested figure, wearing cut-off jeans, was standing immobile at the edge of the water, watching them impassively.

The silence lasted for an endless, heavy moment. 'How ... when did he get here?' Ariel spoke at last, sounding flat, even indifferent.

'A couple of weeks ago.' Laura looked uneasily at her daughter. She had expected amazement, a gush of excitement or anger, but not this odd deadened apathy.

'You should have warned me, Mummy.'

There was another embarrassed pause. 'He asked us not to, Ariel,' her father tried to explain. 'He didn't want you to come back on his account.'

'He knew I was coming home, though. Didn't he?' It was still the same dead, unemotional voice.

'Yes. On a holiday, to recuperate, but not because you felt obliged to see him again.'

'I don't want to see him, Daddy. You must tell him to go away. I just can't take any more!'

Julian Stewart looked stern and uncompromising. 'You must speak to him. If only to give him a chance to explain himself. I know you feel he's betrayed you. But you're wrong. The man couldn't help it. He has no idea what happened to him since he left us.'

Ariel gaped at her father, as if she couldn't quite follow what he was saying to her.

'That's right. He's lost his memory again. So don't go blaming him for keeping away from you all this time.'

They both stared at her aghast as she started laughing. A dry, cheerless laughter which shook her weak body and brought tears of pain to her eyes.

'Stop it, Ariel.' Her father began to shake her. 'You're hysterical. Stop it at once!' He waited until her laughter died.

'This can't be happening, Daddy! I don't believe this,' she mumbled, brokenly. 'You mean to tell me he remembers nothing of——' And then she froze. Kane was no longer standing motionless at the edge of the water. He was walking towards them, his magnificent, lean frame moving in that unhurried, graceful stride, bringing him nearer and nearer to her.

'I won't see him, I can't!' she hissed at her mother. 'I can't face him again, Mummy. Please!'

He heard her, but he kept coming forward, not a muscle moving in his unsmiling, impassive face. She reacted in the only way her shocked senses commanded her: she turned around and tried to escape back into the yacht.

Her father's arm stopped her, almost roughly. 'The least you can do now is be civil to him,' Julian Stewart said quietly. 'You had three years to get over him. I thought you'd grown up since.'

Kane was now standing a few yards away. He made no attempt to come any nearer. She was trapped between him and her unsympathetic parents. They were all looking at her as if she were on the accused stand and they were her judges.

'Hello, Ariel.' He spoke with Chris's dry, unemotional lazy voice. 'You look terrible.'

'Thank you,' she said, hoarsely. 'You, on the other hand, look very well.'

'I do my best.' He gave her his old crooked grin. But his eyes weren't smiling.

Her parents, who were standing there like two pillars of salt, came to life. 'We'll expect you back at the house by seven,' Julian said in his old autocratic manner, as if nothing had happened. 'Don't be late, Ariel.'

They were alone, standing rigidly on the pier, drenched in the breathtaking flames of the setting sun.

'Where will it be?' It was Chris's old infuriating habit of popping up with the most enigmatic questions.

She didn't smile. 'Where will what be?'

'The talk. I don't mind standing here forever, but your legs seem to be a little shaky. Shall we try our old conference office?' She looked at him, blankly. 'The shed, in case you've forgotten.'

'No, I haven't forgotten, and no, not the shed. Anywhere but the shed. What I have to say to you can be said right here and now, Kane.'

'Right, then. Let's hear it.'

'Go away, Kane!'

She might have invited him in for tea, for all the effect her words had on him. 'Well, I'm afraid that may prove a bit difficult,' he said apologetically, frowning slightly. 'I don't know where to go, you see. This is the only place I could think of.'

Despair had drained her of any emotions, except for the dreadful need to get away from him, spare herself any more torment. 'Go back to where you came from then,' she said flatly. 'You should know that much, at least.'

'Mahe,' he answered casually. 'That's where I came from. Exactly where I lost myself three years ago. Don't ask me how I got there or what happened to me in the meantime.' His smile was quite cheerful and amused. 'I really have no idea.'

Her heart was pounding painfully, her whole body aching with a superhuman effort to hold on to her decision. 'I'm sorry, Kane. I'm sorry that you lost your memory again, and I'm sorry I can't be more welcoming. But we can't go back. It's all over.'

'Is it?' he said, sounding mildly intrigued. 'Well, I'd like to discuss that a little further. Do we really have to carry on this conversation standing up like this? We could continue in the cabin, if you really can't face walking to the shed with me.'

He tried to take her arm, but she jerked it free, recoiling from his touch as if burnt by a red-hot iron. 'All right, but you're wasting your time, Kane. I don't want you back.'

The luxuriously equipped main cabin was a far cry from the shabby gentility of the old yacht. It was swathed in the gloom of twilight, but neither took the trouble to turn on the light. 'Sit down, Ariel,' he invited her, as if it were his home. Memory can be so deceptive, she thought to herself. Whatever made her think that Kane wasn't just as arrogant and insufferable as Chris?

His hands came down on her shoulder, pushing her none too gently on to a well upholstered cabin bench. 'Sorry, but you don't look as if your legs could hold you much longer. Now,' he went on, settling comfortably in the seat opposite her but still close enough to make her muscles contract with nervous agitation. He was studying her with Chris's unperturbed, polite interest which was far more threatening than any show of anger. 'Let's take it one by one, shall we? When exactly did you decide to give up on me?'

She braced herself for the coming lie. 'Almost as soon as you left St Patrick. You didn't think I was going to wait forever, did you?'

'Odd,' he said. 'I was given to understand that you'd spent the last three years looking for me.'

'Who told you that, my parents?'

'And Michael, of course.'

'Michael?' In spite of her resolution to keep rigidly calm, her voice rose. 'You've been talking to Michael? He knew you were here?' Kane nodded, taking in her angry response. 'And I suppose you persuaded him, just as you did my parents, to say nothing to me.'

'That's right,' he agreed pleasantly. 'But we'll come back to that later. I instigated this cross-examination, so I'll finish. You must agree that I have the right to know what has happened over the last few weeks to make me dispensable all of a sudden?'

Her nails were digging painfully into the palms of

her hands. 'I've been ill ... it changed me. I don't know how, it just did.'

'I don't believe you, Ariel.' His voice lost its calm laziness as he stood up, towering above her. 'I can think of only two possible answers. One, that you've decided you can't rely on a man who keeps losing his memory whenever the wind changes. Is that it, Ariel? Have you given up on me because I'm a hopeless amnesiac?' He jerked her angrily from her chair and held her up, ignoring her weak efforts to get away from him. 'Answer me, damn you!'

'No!' she shouted back at the cold mask of his anger, blurred by the flowing tears of fear and misery. 'That's not it! I couldn't care less about that. I never did, and you know it as well as I do!'

'Yes, I guess I do. So what is it, then?' he said more gently now. 'Don't keep me guessing, sweetheart. Or I'll have to use another way of getting at the truth.'

She felt a surge of giggles rise up. He didn't really think that she would be taken in by that act. Kane wasn't capable of violence any more than Chris was. 'You mean, you'll revert to physical violence?'

'Physical yes, but not necessarily violence,' he answered gravely, and his mouth came down to claim hers.

She didn't try to push him away, knowing how pitiful her attempt would prove against his deceptively light hold. She just kept her eyes open, bracing her will-power to ward off her body's response. But she was just as powerless against Kane's unhurried, confident assailment of her senses as she was of Chris's. As his lips and tongue kept storming her weakening resolve, she began to panic, and with one, strong push, managed to pull out of his arms.

Her whole being was shaking as she stood back and faced him. Nothing on earth would make her go again through the agony of loving this man who was fated to live as two. She couldn't bear to see him living the torment of a double life, torn by jealousy, torturing her love with his doubts. She was poison to him as he was to her. They were doomed to love each other for ever and yet never find peace and fulfilment in their love. And she had to save both him and herself from that inescapable hell.

'So, my love, where do we go from here?' He grinned at her, utterly calm and unconcerned, waving away her violent rejection of his kiss as if it were a mildly annoying fly.

'Nowhere,' she said quietly. 'Nowhere, Kane. I love you, I never stopped loving you, but I love someone else just as much.'

He still had that grin on his face. 'Do you now? So what are you doing here on St Patrick? Why aren't you with him, wherever he is?'

'For the same reason I refuse to be with you. I'd rather have neither than be torn apart having to choose between you.'

She heard Kane sigh softly, but she could detect neither sadness nor resignation in the dark blue eyes which were boring into hers mercilessly. Only a curious widening of the pupils, and an almost imperceptible relaxation of the unyielding, handsome face.

'Yes,' he said simply, and something in the low, pleasant voice started an alarm bell going which was piercing her baffled senses. It was as if Chris, not Kane, was taunting her misery with that calculated, unperturbed calm. 'That's just what Michael said.'

Ariel tore her gaze away from his. She couldn't let him taunt her any further, whether innocently or wilfully. Her senses were now tingling with encroaching danger. 'So if you have any feelings left for me, Kane, please . . . do what the other one did and go away. Just leave me alone!' she finished, listlessly.

Her words rang through the curiously still cabin. The silence seemed to go on for ever.

And then he spoke again, and now she was sure that it wasn't Kane speaking, but Chris. 'And would you have said the same thing to me if I had asked you to marry me that Sunday night, at the Mayfair rest— Easy, Ariel!'

She didn't hear the rest, her knees gave in under her

and she began to sink down to the floor. But his strong arms caught her just in time.

'Hell, sweetheart. What a stupid brute I am,' she heard him muttering angrily against her cold cheek as he picked her up in his arms.

He carried her to the deck, away from the stifling air of the cabin, and settled her on the wooden bench, supporting her with one arm as his other hand kept stroking her icy face. 'I'm sorry, sweetheart. It was a stupid, cruel masquerade, but I had to know.'

'Chris?' she murmured. 'I mean, Kane . . . Oh God, I don't know what I mean. Which one are you?'

'Chris if you like, Kane if you prefer your own name for me. I'm both here, if you know what *I* mean. And, if you want my opinion, I wouldn't have either one of us—of me, that is. We're both insensitive bloody fools. But then it's hardly surprising, since we're after all one and the same man.'

She didn't understand a word he was saying. Her hands were tracing the strong lines of his face, as if to reassure herself by their familiar shape that she was indeed touching both Kane and Chris.

'You know about Kane? I mean, about Chris?' She kept mumbling questions which made no sense whatsoever, and certainly didn't require any answers. 'And you've been here all this time?'

'That's right. Ever since I left London. Though I could have kicked myself for leaving you when Michael cabled us here about your illness. I almost flew back then, except that he assured me that you were on the mend now and would be coming here soon. We both thought it best if we met here.'

'So Michael and you conspired against me again?' The indignant words were somehow belied by the way she kept kissing his face, his bare chest. 'You could have spared me that last final torture, Chris.'

'You and me, sweetheart, but I had to do it. For both our sakes. We both had to know for sure where you stood with either Kane or Chris.' He gripped her face and brought it up so that he could look into her eyes. 'And now we know, don't we? Just tell me again what you said then.'

She knew, without a moment's thought, what he meant. 'I love you so much I think I'll burst!' she quoted obediently, repeating the words she had said to him in the villa, on their last night together. 'In fact, I think I have done already. I feel as if I've burst out of my body and am now floating somewhere in Never-Neverland.'

It was a lie, her body was still very much with her as Chris's kiss, deep and endless, persisted to reassure her.

'That's enough, Ariel.' He pushed her away finally, as their pulses started racing again. 'We'll have to stop now. It's almost seven, and your father will send us to bed without food if we're late for dinner.'

'Let him,' she muttered, burying her head in his chest, cooled by the evening breeze. 'I can't bear to share you with anyone right now.'

He smiled down at her. 'Could you bear not to see your home for a few more days then?'

'I could bear anything as long as I don't wake up to find either of you gone!' She sat up, in a panic. 'Where are you going?'

'Only to radio your father and tell him we're off.'

'No, don't! Oh damn you, Chris. Don't leave me now!' Like a terrified child, she stumbled after him, holding on to his arm. And then she registered what he had just said. 'Off where?'

'Sailing. That was the original idea, if you remember.' He laughed at her perplexed expression and taking advantage of her momentary freeze, he quickly walked away to the deck cabin and began fiddling with the radio.

'Julian?' she heard him say. 'You'd better start dinner without us. We won't be back for a few days yet . . .' Her father's voice came flooding in in unintelligible metallic crackles. 'Yes, I think it is. The sooner the better. Except that . . . hold on a second, will you?'

Turning to her, he let his hand rest on her head,

brushing her short hair back away from her forehead, in an old familiar gesture. 'It's the same old problem, love.'

'What is?' she asked, frantic suddenly.

'I'm afraid I went ahead and took your answer for granted, Ariel,' he mumbled, somewhat sheepish. 'And I can't even promise I'll ever change. So, you'd better think it over before you rush into anything.'

Ariel's hands curled into fists. She had reached the end of her tether. 'Think what over?' she hissed, itching to hit him. 'What the hell are you talking about, Chris?'

Her father's exasperated voice filled the small cabin with impatient demands for attention. 'All right, all right, give me a second, Julian. God, what an impatient family you all are!' he groaned as he pulled her to him. 'I'd better make it quick, then. Will you marry me, Ariel?'

She wasn't given a chance to nod, let alone find her voice. 'Yes, it's all right,' he returned to the radio. 'We'll be back in time for the wedding, don't worry. As soon as you can organise it.' He listened for a second and then spoke solemnly. 'Well, you may know your daughter, Julian. But you ought to know me as well by now. Honourable to a fault.'

To her amazement, she heard her father's dry, off-key voice break into an energetic rendition of 'He'll always be an Englishman'.

'You mean, you would have remembered everything if I had only told you the truth the very first time we met?' Ariel asked wonderingly a few hours later, cuddling closely against him. They were far away from St Patrick and the Seychelles now, the yacht rocking gently in the middle of the ocean, and there was nothing around them but the velvety darkness of the night.

'I don't think so,' he answered gravely. 'Much as I regret the hard time you have been giving us both by lying to me about not having known me before, I think you were right to let me struggle with my memory alone.'

'But you said that you remembered everything when you heard me cry Kane's name when...' She suddenly felt awkward. 'You know, when you and I——'

He didn't taunt her. 'That was the final push, my love. It wouldn't have helped if I hadn't already been half way there. You did call me by that name on your first night, remember? And it was a pretty shattering jolt, I can tell you that. But I've had so many false alarms before that I rejected it as just another pathetic quirk of my poor memory. Like your laughter, and your quick temper, and your endless chatter, and those elfin eyes.' His arm tightened around her deliciously alert body. 'And your name, of course.'

'Oh, yes. I forgot about that. Thank you for naming your yacht after me,' she murmured, pushing her hand under his soft loose jumper to feel the texture of his skin. He was now fully dressed against the fresh night air. 'I wish I'd known then that you had at least retained the memory of my name.'

'Yes, that was the most suspicious coincidence of all. There are very few people who know the name of my yacht but since you came from the Seychelles, I was sure you had seen it somewhere and assumed the name as part of your plan to trick me ... and you'd better stop that right away,' he ended wryly, slapping her invading hand away. 'Please, Ariel. Stop tempting me.' True to his promise to her father, Chris kept her at arm's length on the upper deck though she knew well that she wouldn't let him keep his word much longer.

'Oh, excuse me,' she answered demurely and scrambled away, leaving a few feet between them, just as she had done during those first months of his stay on St Patrick, after he had warned her not to provoke him any more. 'Is that better?'

He groaned ruefully, and pulled her back to him. 'Don't overdo it now.'

'Whatever you say, Sir,' she assured him and settled back against his warm, broad chest. 'So when did you realise that I wasn't hiding behind an assumed name?'

'Oh, when I looked in your passport and . . .'

'Where did you find it?' She stopped him and giggled when she saw his look. 'Don't tell me. You went through my bag, or ransacked my room?'

He nodded, not particularly shamefaced. 'Sorry, darling, I just had to know,' he said simply.

'Honestly, Chris,' she became indignant, 'that was a mean thing to do. When I think of the trouble I'd taken not to revert to any dishonourable measures. I could have easily blackmailed you, pumped Marjorie or Daria for information. I've been so honest . . .'

He gave a bark of sardonic laughter. 'You honest? Good Lord, Ariel. You never stopped insulting my intelligence with your transparent lies, inventing all those outrageous stories . . . In fact, it was precisely because you were so bad at it that it dawned on me that you might not be just another pretender, trying to hitch-hike on my buried past.'

'Instead you deduced that I was the true author of the novel, come to demand my share,' she mocked him.

He wasn't amused. 'I couldn't care less about the novel by then. I was too incensed by your obsession with that mysterious Kane.' He looked angrily at her laughing face. 'You think it's funny, do you?' He pushed her against the wooden deck and punished her with a long deep kiss, moulding her body into his own long frame. 'You try and live with a black gaping hole,' he said drily when he released her at last. 'Do you know how it feels to live day in day out, flogging your memory to death trying to understand what makes you so cold and untouched, why you shut yourself off from the most alluring creatures, including you!'

'Or Cynthia? Or Daria?' she retorted with the same anger.

'Yes, why not? I could do worse, you know,' he agreed readily, punishing her for her earlier mockery. 'I had no idea what it was that held me back. I just knew there was someone who had total control over my life even if I couldn't remember her face or her name or anything about her.'

They lapsed into silence as memories brought back all the anguish and bewilderment. And then another thought occurred to her. 'Wait, Chris. You told Marjorie that you'd decided to marry me even before our last night together. Was it because you . . . I mean, were you——'

'No.' As always he could read her thoughts before she could put them into fumbling words. 'I didn't just give up on my old dream, if that's what you're asking. I just knew that I loved you as much, perhaps even more than that shadowy phantom. I felt I could forget it in my love for you and I was sure it was deep and strong enough to make you forget the man I thought was my absent rival. I actually told you so, if not in so many words.' His voice became accusing, almost sullen. 'You might have told me then that I could stop worrying about him.'

'Why should I have?' she answered caustically. 'You made it sound like a business deal: My ghost in exchange for yours, I'm willing if you are, that sort of thing. You were so beastly, so arrogant . . .'

He wasn't going to give in that easily. 'All right, then. If you insist on competing, what about that time on the Heath? You could see that I was going out of my mind with half-aroused memories. And instead of telling me the truth, you just kept taunting me with Kane . . .'

'Don't you accuse *me* of taunting you!' she burst out, shocked to hear how wrong she had been about his feelings for her then. 'What about you? You just sat there, as smug as a cat who's just caught a mouse, informing me that you'd deigned to find me worthy as a substitute for your lost love. What was I supposed to do, kneel down and thank you for agreeing to take me to bed?'

As always, her quick temper only managed to amuse him. 'It would have saved us both a lot of time. All I needed was to hold your naked body in my arms, feel that wonderful abandon as you gave yourself to me . . . Oh, my love,' he groaned, his hands cupping her face so that he could look into her eyes, even now shaken by the memory of that moment. 'I can't tell you what it was like. It didn't happen in a sudden burst. It wasn't a devastating shock at all. When you were struggling with the buttons of my shirt, muttering away, trying to undress me, clumsy and delicious as you have always been with me, it was as if the last shred of a misty veil had been removed from my mind and I just knew that I was the Kane you were crying for and that you were my love, my only love, and that time had just stopped still for three long years, and everything was right again. Oh, hell, I could have died with love for you at that moment.'

And as if trying to wipe off the agony of having to relinquish his love on that night, he pulled her head down to bury his thoughts in her kiss. And as she felt him shuddering with the uncontrollable surge of his love and desire for her, she pushed him away and stood up.

'Please, Chris,' she said tightly. 'Don't you start now. I'm a human being too, you know.'

In one light leap, he was up on his feet, and he scooped her effortlessly into his arms. 'Well, so am I. So to hell with it, darling. Let's go below. You haven't seen the master cabin yet, have you?' She shook her head and he went on to explain as he carried her down the narrow steps. 'Very narrow, I'm afraid. No question of your staying on your side of the bed. I think you'll like it.'

He held nothing back now as he swept her with him towards the fulfilment of their love, abandoning his expert, confident love-making in the savage impatient hunger for the joy of their reunion after three lonely and barren years.

'Sorry, my love. For once it was me rushing you instead of the other way round,' he muttered into her breasts, as he lay in her arms, gasping for breath. 'I wonder what Julian would say if he knew. Honourable to a fault, my foot!'

'You can always blame it on me. My parents know I can't be trusted,' she comforted him, solemnly. Then she shuddered as another unbearably painful memory surged up. 'Why didn't you take me on that last night at the villa, Chris? Why did you leave me?' Her arms tightened around his back, convulsively. 'You knew you were Kane, you knew I loved no one else, yet you went away.'

Chris didn't answer for a moment. Then he moved away from her, putting a distance between them. 'Yes, I knew it. But I wasn't any more the lost man you'd brought back to life, and moulded into your own romantic dream. I was Chris Donahue, Ariel. A man with a past and a future, burdened with responsibilities, a huge, demanding business, not to mention a very unpleasant bunch of hangers-on. And,' he stopped her before she could protest, 'I wasn't a very nice man to be with, as you never failed to inform me.'

'Well, you weren't! You were arrogant and unyielding and enigmatic and insufferable, but so was Kane!'

'Perhaps,' he conceded. 'But I had to be sure that you loved me, the real me. Not a ghost from the past. That's why I orchestrated this ridiculous farce, pretending to be the amnesiac Kane again.' He chuckled smugly. 'Both Michael and your parents warned me that you wouldn't be taken in by it. You were, though, weren't you?'

'Well, don't be so smug, Chris. You've drained me of any sense, playing hot and cold on me as you kept doing. I wonder though,' she suddenly had another thought, 'I wonder what you would have done if I had fallen into your arms the moment I saw you and taken you back. As Kane. I almost did, you know. It was the most difficult thing I've ever done, telling you to go away.'

He sat up. 'I wondered about that myself. I suppose I would have carried it on for a while, making it up as we went along, slowly bringing you around to accept me as Chris as well as Kane. And meanwhile, as long as I had you with me, I was quite happy to take it one life at a time.'

He was up, threading his long, lean leg into Kane's

tatty, cut-off jeans. 'Where are you off to now?' she demanded, baffled by the sudden attack of energy.

'Work,' he announced calmly. 'You too, lazybones. Come on. We have hardly five days to finish that bloody adaptation.'

'Why? We have all the time in the world now,' she groaned.

'I don't. Once we're married, it's back to real life with me.'

'The Donahue empire?'

'Among other things like taking care of my wife, bringing up our children, that sort of thing. I'm leaving all that creative imagination to you, my darling. Mine is going to be too busy finding ways of keeping you happy, body and soul. So, come on. Back to work!'

'Chris,' she said patiently. 'It's three in the morning. Don't you think you're exaggerating?'

He looked at his watch, rather taken aback. 'So it is. Oh, well, I guess it is a bit late. To start working, that is. On the other hand, it's just the right time to resume where we left off and Julian will just have to forgive me again.' He was already out of his clothes and back beside her in the narrow double bed. 'Come here, love.'

And slowly, blissfully, he once again carried her away on their long journey into the future, glowing with the deep, unshaken certainty that this time it would not be one life at a time, but a whole, united lifetime.

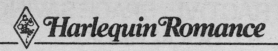
❧ Harlequin Romance

Coming Next Month

2803   A THOUSAND ROSES Bethany Campbell
The tough-talking daughter of a professional wrestler isn't
intimidated by a miserly Scrooge who tries to lay claim to her
home at Christmas. But the strange tantalizing force drawing
them together unnerves her.

2804   THE HERON QUEST Charlotte Lamb
For a writer and a TV producer who set out to make a
documentary together, love isn't out of the question. But
according to him, marriage is....

2805   AT DAGGERS DRAWN Margaret Mayo
A surgery nurse has a rough time convincing her new boss in
the Lake District that she didn't take the job to be near his
brother. Then when she does convince him, an old boyfriend
turns up and ruins her hopes of marriage.

2806   CAPTURE A SHADOW Leigh Michaels
When a New York editor's top-selling romance author quits,
she sets off on a frantic search with only a pen name and a
Midwest town post-office box to go on. Luckily, an
outrageously appealing local author joins the hunt.

2807   THE WAITING MAN Jeneth Murrey
A widow and her son, heir to the family fortune, are tracked
down by her grandfather's handsome henchman. He has his
own ax to grind with her tyrannical grandfather. But is
marriage the answer?

2808   TWO WEEKS TO REMEMBER Betty Neels
If two weeks could turn into a lifetime, then a typist would
have more than memories of her thrilling trip to Norway with a
brilliant doctor. She'd have a bright, shining future as his wife!

Available in December wherever paperback books are sold,
or through Harlequin Reader Service.

In the U.S.
P.O. Box 1397
Buffalo, N.Y.
14240-1397

In Canada
P.O. Box 603
Fort Erie, Ontario
L2A 9Z9